Praise for

They Were Here Before Us

"Imagine Richard Adams devoured by Clive Barker, and Barker devoured by the beetles that ate of Poe, and now the beetles tell their stories, and every last one of them breaks your heart. Each of these tales is bloodier, darker, and grander than the last. Eric LaRocca's voice—so evocative, so original, so urgent—is one for the ages."
— ANDY DAVIDSON, Multiple Bram Stoker Award® finalist and author of *The Hollow Kind*

"Horror is sometimes meant to wield a razor, to hurt, to scar, to appall. Eric LaRocca's *They Were Here Before Us* does all that. I was shocked, dismayed, angered, disgusted, and I applaud Eric for taking me there."
— JOHN F.D. TAFF, Multiple Bram Stoker Award® finalist and author of *The Fearing*

"Eric LaRocca's *They Were Here Before Us* is a disquieting piece of work. Readers will live with this one for a while."
— LAIRD BARRON, Bram Stoker® and Shirley Jackson Award-winning author of *Swift to Chase*

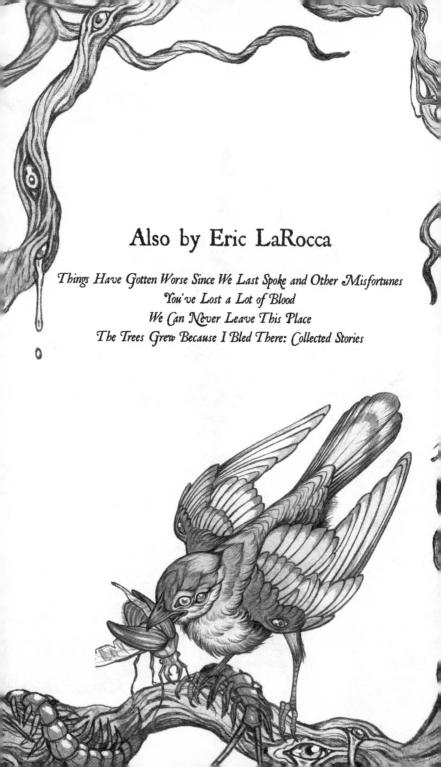

Also by Eric LaRocca

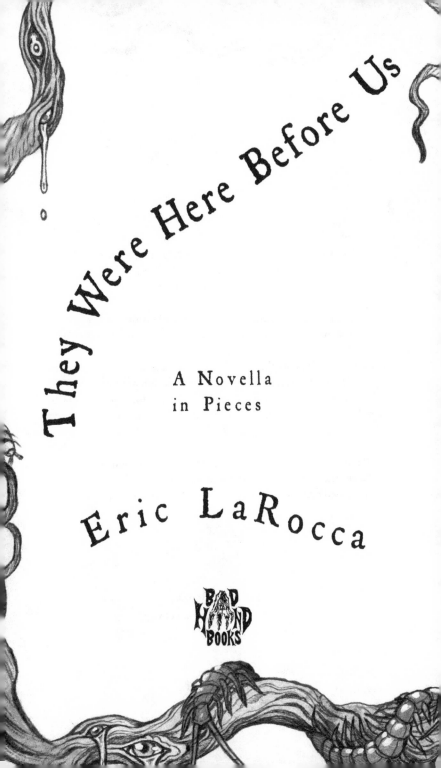

They Were Here Before Us

A Novella
in Pieces

Eric LaRocca

BAD HAND BOOKS

THEY WERE HERE BEFORE US: A NOVELLA IN PIECES
Copyright © 2022 by Eric LaRocca
Print ISBN: 979-8-218-01532-9

Cover & interior artwork by Caitlin Hackett | CaitlinHackett.com
Cover & interior design by Todd Keisling | Dullington Design Co.

Bad Hand Books
www.badhandbooks.com

For Clive,
Thank you for the sights you've shown me.

A Word of Warning

How do you do?

Mr. LaRocca feels it would be a little unkind to present this book without just a word of friendly warning.

We are about to unfold *They Were Here Before Us:* a novella stitched together in pieces—short stories, vignettes, novelettes—and meant to be consumed and considered as a thematically unified whole.

It is one of the strangest tales ever told. It deals with two of the great mysteries of our earthy existence: nature and love. How does one inform the other? How does one encroach upon the other? How does one destroy the other?

I think it will thrill you. It may enrage you. It might even nauseate you.

So, if any of you feel you do not wish to subject your nerves to stories containing graphic depictions of dismemberment, disembowelment, interspecies necrophilia, heavily implied interspecies love affairs or art-as-torture, now is your chance to...

Well...we've warned you.

Doug Murano
Editor-in-Chief
Bad Hand Books

They Were Here Before Us

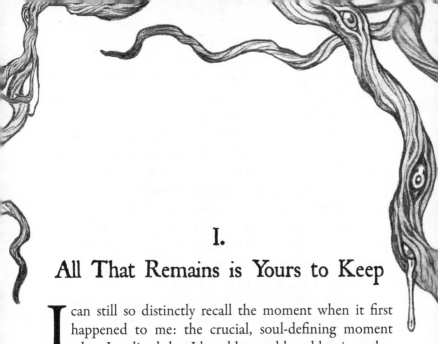

I.

All That Remains is Yours to Keep

I can still so distinctly recall the moment when it first happened to me: the crucial, soul-defining moment when I realized that I loved her and loved her in such a way that I understood I could never fully possess her as I had always intended.

Perhaps "love" wasn't exactly the right word.

In fact, perhaps "love" was far too benign of a word given the intensity of my feelings for her.

After all, the word "love" usually implies that there are two consenting individuals, both capable of giving and receiving respect, admiration, esteem, tenderness. Though she might have once loved me—might have cared for me, nurtured me the way I had hoped, the way I had dreamed and wanted—that opportunity was now decidedly nonexistent, considering the fact that she was dead and had been dead for several weeks when my parents first stumbled upon her corpse in a shallow ditch not far from a busy motorway.

For my siblings and I, she was our first cradle, our bassinet—the very framework of our existence. All thirty of us were more than grateful for her body as we had already begun to make our home, our refuge, our haven from the

delicate intricacy of her cadaver. Her nostrils were our secret passageways where we could lose ourselves, where we could wander aimlessly until we were found. Her lips were our velvet cushions, luxurious pillows where we could sleep and dream until our next feeding. Her pried-open, ever-vigilant eyes—our relaxing sauna, far more preferable and far more tepid than any mountain spring. Her flesh—our holy communion, our sacred bond, the thing that kept us tethered as a family.

We had gorged ourselves on her body's offerings day in and day out, our parents sometimes feeding us with bits of her they had taken and tucked away for safekeeping. For a family of beetles, we were keenly aware just how fortunate, how privileged we were to maintain such a luxurious environment. Our parents often regaled us with tales of former residences where they had to make do with the corpse of a shrew or the rotted body of a small possum. To find a human so healthy and in such excellent condition as she hadn't been dead for too long was a work of pure magic, an object of enchantment.

Of course, as I look back on the moment when it first occurred to me that I loved her and loved her in earnest, I comprehended that those feelings, those sentiments, were present as long as I had been a living thing—a measly insect that crawls, creeps, and chews its way through the brawn of existence.

After all, her body was all I had ever known.

Still, as I looked back and recalled the moment I had first described these feelings as "love," I realized I had always been innately curious as to how such a radiant, mesmerizing creature ended up flat on her back in a small ditch hidden away in the darker corner of a lonely thicket. I couldn't help but wonder what had happened to her. I wondered why she always appeared frightened, her eyes and mouth permanently open as if forever caught in the moment of some terrible surprise. I wondered why parts of her silky auburn hair were now crusted black with bits of dried blood as dark as motor oil.

I yearned to know her secrets. Perhaps the most beguiling and mystifying one had to do with the fact that her stomach was always distended. Our parents assured us that this was normal and that all different types of bodies often decompose in such a way that causes them to bloat obscenely or inflate with gases.

Regardless, I will always recall the moment when I was crawling my way across her belly and I felt a distinct sense of affection, an indescribable feeling of joy and how it seemed to overcome me almost instantly. It wasn't because I felt safe or because I knew my parents cared for their brood in such a way that meant we would never want for anything as long as we lived. Although those feelings were quite frequent and were well founded given the love we were afforded, the thought that suddenly came crashing into my mind had nothing to do with that.

It was a tremendous, remarkable moment—when I realized that I loved her and loved her for far more than the mere use of her body as my home, my shelter. It wasn't long until I found myself scurrying across her face and weaving in between her nostrils, playing a game with myself that I knew she might appreciate if she were able to see me in all my glory.

A curious part of me wondered if she might be disgusted with me, if she might despise me for all I had taken from her or simply detest me for the fact that I was a mere bug—a small, pathetic insect undeserving of such beauty, such magnificence, such grace. After all, my parents had ravaged her and made a nest, a viable home in her body for their starving, insatiable young.

To her, we might have been monsters. Perhaps we were. But she didn't object. How could she?

After I realized the extent of my feelings— that I was deeply infatuated with this poor, young woman who had been robbed of youth, beauty, and any semblance of proper human dignity—I found myself unsettled by the idea of using her corpse as my nourishment. The very thought of feeding on her, shitting on her, fucking on her repulsed me unlike anything else. These feelings of revulsion, pity, and disgust compelled me to stop feeding regularly and it was then that I began to starve myself in order to save her.

It wasn't a noticeable change at first, but soon, my brothers and sisters noticed I wasn't gorging like them at mealtime. I simply explained that I hadn't been hungry lately and that I wasn't feeling well. These excuses bought me some time, but not enough time to evade the suspicions of my parents who had noticed an unfavorable change in my appetite.

Accusations were hurled at me—words like "ungrateful," "immature," and "spoiled."

If only they knew how I truly felt, I thought to myself, luxuriating in the imaginary warmth of my one true love. *If only they knew how I had found the very thing that matters more to me than life itself.*

When I was feeling particularly despondent and aching for a semblance of love or affection, I considered how I might refer to her—my immortal starlight, my everlasting beloved. After all, I couldn't keep calling her "my beloved" in my head as I knew the thought would eventually slip out and my parents might hear. I wondered what I should name her. For some inexplicable reason, to me, she resembled the quiet, proper demureness of an Agatha.

I decided that's what I would call her.

I would refer to her only as Agatha.

It felt silly at first—a mere insect deciding the name of a human being, a grown woman who presumably had a life filled with loved ones before she met her unfortunate and gruesome demise. Although it could be argued that she had more foes than friends given the fact she had been reclining in the ditch for several weeks and I'd not seen or heard any evidence of a search.

Are they looking for her? I wondered. *Will somebody eventually come and take my beloved Agatha away from me?*

I couldn't allow that to happen. I'd sooner die than see her ladled from this ditch to be buried properly inside a casket.

After a few weeks passed, several of my brothers and sisters began to sprout wings and ferry themselves away from the home our parents had made for us.

I lingered.

I had no intention or plans of leaving. I think, on some level, my parents were acutely aware of that. Regardless, they were quick to ask me when I'd be parting from them, when I'd be brazen enough to leave the nest and find a home of my own—another corpse where I could roost with a beetle of the opposite sex and mate in order to complete the life cycle. To me, the notion of it sounded excruciating. I wanted nothing to do with other beetles, other members of my own kind. I only wanted to be with her, my true love.

My darling Agatha.

After weeks of coaxing me to depart, my parents gave up and flitted away to find a new nest. Whether they were exhausted with me or desperate to find newer, more comfortable accommodations, I was never fully certain. Despite my doubt, the moment I had been yearning for finally came. I was alone with my beloved Agatha. She belonged to me and me alone. Our time alone was short lived, however, as others soon arrived— various kinds of ants, worms, and maggots.

Though I strained to explain to them how Agatha was a

rarity—a precious gem that must be protected at all costs—the other insects and eaters of carrion would have none of it. They paid me little mind, scouring her body and gorging themselves on her as she continued to deteriorate—to rot—right before my eyes. I apologized to her day in and day out, assuring her that they would leave when they finally had their fill.

Then, something remarkable happened.

Something truly incomprehensible and unexpected.

I woke one morning and peered out from the corridor of her nostrils where I often slept, and it was then that I noticed something dark and wet lying in the dirt between where Agatha's open legs met.

There, on the ground, was a dead newborn, its rubbery skin glistening as if freshly lacquered with oil.

It was about as small as a baby rodent—curled up as if attempting to make itself smaller, as if willing itself to remain as precious and as delicate as possible in a world that so desperately wanted to harm it. I couldn't help but notice a blood-slimed rope attached to the newborn and coiling up beneath Agatha's dirt-caked skirt, as if the two were forever connected, as if nothing could ever tear mother and child apart.

Not even death.

Several of the ant colonies that had overtaken Agatha's body had already realized the arrival of the little corpse and were beginning to migrate from Agatha to the deceased little one lying further down inside the bowl of the trench. It wasn't long before the tiny thing's carcass was forever lost in a blur, a violent swarm of insects making their way across its soft, pink skin. For several moments, I watched quietly as maggots burrowed between the child's eyelids, as worms slithered between its elastic band lips.

I did not feel pity or sadness or even disgust while watching the other insects crowd over the poor child's body and begin to devour, boring into the precious thing as if its skin were wet cotton. To me, the child deserved this. This was what I wanted. After all, I wanted to be alone with Agatha more than anything. That's what I wanted most of all. But a child. *A child?* That would ruin everything for me, everything I had so meticulously planned, everything I had so desperately yearned for and hoped for.

So, instead of begging the others to stop what they were doing as I had done with Agatha, I did no such thing as they swarmed the newborn.

In fact, I encouraged them.

I egged them on, cheered them on to eat as much as possible until they were fit to burst, until they were as disgustingly bloated as a tick on a newborn fawn. I shouted at them, contended that they wouldn't be fit to eat the Imperial son of a Sultan considering their lackluster performance so far. And they ate. And ate. And ate. And ate.

Finally, after weeks, all that was left of the poor child was a dark stain—a trail of glinting viscera, a lost murmur of what had once been but was unquestionably no more. All that remained didn't even resemble the remnants of a human life. It was an abomination—a cruel, sadistic joke played by Mother Nature.

After more weeks passed and the weeks bled into months, the throng of hungry insects gathered on Agatha's body began to dissipate as they had finally had their fill. I kept watch, making certain they didn't take too much from her, making certain that what remained of her beauty and refinement was left untouched, undisturbed.

It wasn't long before I was once again completely alone with my beloved Agatha, my sweet woman of many mysteries. I didn't chastise her for keeping such an enormous secret from me. Nor did I condemn her for making me suffer by the sheer fact that so many others wanted her, needed her. But certainly not the same way I wanted and needed her.

As I made my way toward her, crawling up her extremity knitted with rot, I found myself puzzled by her. It was somehow as if we were suddenly able to communicate with one another. She did not welcome me as I had anticipated she might. She did not rejoice at my arrival, did not welcome me with the reverence, the kindness, the tenderness I had imagined for so long—the intimacy I had expected when we were finally left alone.

Instead, she simply lay there. Without comment. Without adoration. Without anything.

It was then I realized the truth—she hated me. Despised me. She loathed me for what I had allowed to happen to her child. In some quiet part of her she had expected me to protect her baby the way I had always strained to protect her. I knew this to be true. I didn't need her to say it. She despised me for my insect-like callousness, my uncaring attitude, my willingness to allow her precious child to be devoured right between her legs.

Even worse, she was judging me.

Her eyes—listless egg yolks secured in hollow sockets—fixed themselves upon me and glared at me with such unreserved contempt, such condemnation.

"Please, Agatha," I begged her. "I wanted you to love only me."

But she wouldn't listen. She received my pleas, my explanations without comment.

For the first time in my life, I felt betrayed. I felt shame for what I had done—the horrible thing I had let happen to that innocent, dead newborn.

However, what hurt the most was her glaring, her unreserved staring as she silently condemned me in this life and the one to come.

It was then that I decided I must do something that could not be undone—something that I had quietly dreaded while the other insects had their way with her, something I was keen to supervise every day to make certain they were healthy and in proper place.

Her eyes.

I realized that something must be done about the woman's hate-filled eyes.

Without any further hesitation, I made my way to her left eye. I stared at it for a moment, quietly appraising what I should do and what would be the most painless way of putting her out of such misery. With a swift motion, I skirted beneath the flesh of her eyelid and began burrowing through the bulb of her eye. It burst like a sweet jelly in my mouth. I kept eating until her eye was completely gone and I curled inside its empty socket.

Then when I had finished gorging on her left eye, I crawled onto her right one and began feasting on that as well.

Finally, two empty sunken pits stared back at me.

My work was completed. I had done the very thing I had promised I would never do again—feed from my beloved Agatha. Now she could never judge me, could never loathe me the way I imagined she might.

She would always love me, would always care for me while I coiled myself inside her skull and waited for the dawn to break, for the sky to split open with light.

"You feel like home, Agatha" I whispered to her.

Of course, she said nothing. What was there to say?

Over the days, months, years others might come. There might be scavengers, other animals that might tear her away and drag her back to the sanctity of their mountain dens. I always knew this. But they would never fully possess her the way I have. To them, she would be nothing more than a refuge, a meal, a transitory place to bury the larvae of their precious offspring.

To me, she was so much more.

Even better, they would never have her eyes the same way I had them. Even though they might dream, they might yearn, they might pine for a semblance of the same gift I had received, it will never be so for them the way it was for me.

Her eyes will always belong to me.

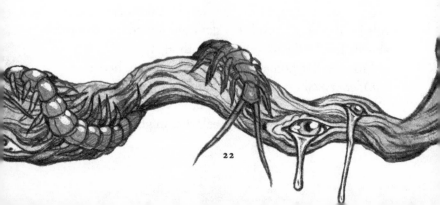

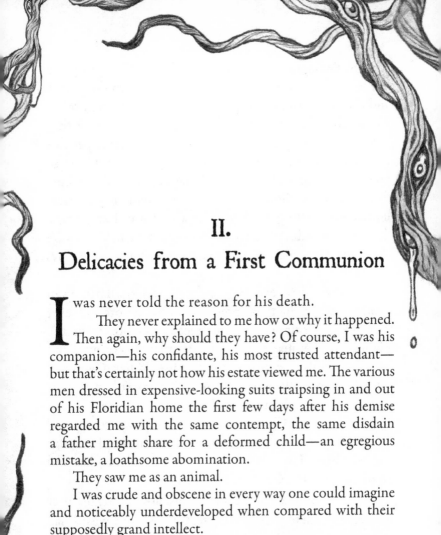

II.

Delicacies from a First Communion

I was never told the reason for his death.

They never explained to me how or why it happened. Then again, why should they have? Of course, I was his companion—his confidante, his most trusted attendant—but that's certainly not how his estate viewed me. The various men dressed in expensive-looking suits traipsing in and out of his Floridian home the first few days after his demise regarded me with the same contempt, the same disdain a father might share for a deformed child—an egregious mistake, a loathsome abomination.

They saw me as an animal.

I was crude and obscene in every way one could imagine and noticeably underdeveloped when compared with their supposedly grand intellect.

"Chimps are usually quite smart," I heard one of them mutter as they passed the small enclosure where I had been sequestered since his body was discovered in the third-floor parlor. "It almost looks as if he can understand us. Doesn't it?"

"I'm surprised Edgar kept that beast in the house with him," the other one remarked, lordly sneering at me. "Disgusting. It looks as if it has a mind to chew our faces off."

Yes. Perhaps they were right. Perhaps I had considered leaping out of my enclosure, attaching myself to their faces, and clawing until I could peel the skin from them in thick, bloody threads. But I knew for certain that was what they expected of me. I had never been one to surrender to people's expectations. That was what made living with Edgar so grand, so wonderfully divine. He never expected anything from me. Even though our means to communicate were limited considering the fact I was what I was, I knew for a fact he never subscribed to the notion that he held a station above me. He made it certain that we were equals and always would be.

However, his lover, Cy, did not feel similarly. Even though Edgar had adopted me long before he ever met the tan-skinned, dimple-faced socialite from the Hamptons, Cy made every effort to let me know that I was an unwelcome guest in the house. When Cy stayed over, I was not allowed to sleep in the master bedroom as was usually my custom when Edgar and I had the house to ourselves. When Cy stayed over, I was always segregated to a small crate near the house's basement-level laundry room. There, I would usually have a small blanket and some rations that Cy would prepare for me.

I often wondered if Edgar knew just how poorly his lover treated me. There were, of course, times when I wish I had the capacity to ask him. Moreover, there were times when I wondered if Cy knew of the connection Edgar and I shared together—the love that tethered us and that could not be broken even by the arrival of death.

However, now that Edgar was gone, I couldn't help but wonder what might become of me. Naturally, I expected the executors of his estate would parcel everything away until all his earthly possessions were scattered to the winds. As much as I detested to acknowledge the fact, I was considered one of the dead man's mere possessions—relics from a departed era to be discarded, to be scattered as if I were nothing more than a useless artifact from a forgotten civilization. Perhaps that's what I was. Perhaps I possessed the same usefulness of a dead language. After all, that was what Cy thought of me. But I had to do whatever I could to prove him wrong.

"What's to be done with the chimp?" one of the men asked Cy as they passed by my enclosure again.

I straightened a little while I sunned myself underneath the glow of the afternoon Pensacola sun.

"What's the damned thing named?" another one asked. "Edgar always called him something."

"Enkidu," Cy muttered.

I perked up, my ears pinning at the sound of my name.

"Named after one of Gilgamesh's companions," he said.

One of the gentlemen dressed in expensive black circled the small outdoor enclosure where I was secluded. I waited until he was about a foot or so from the railing that separated the concourse from the enclosure, and then I lifted my ass into the air and defecated right in front of him. Out of my peripheral vision, I noticed some of the other gentlemen glancing away in visible distress, violently fanning the air as if to cure some of the horrible smell of chimpanzee shit. Cy seemed to receive the spectacle without comment, without objection. After all, he was accustomed to my disobedience.

"You're seriously considering keeping this creature?" one of the men asked Cy. "A zoo might be far more preferable."

"I don't have much of a choice," Cy explained, his eyes lowering and his voice quivering a little. "Edgar made me promise that I would take care of Enkidu if anything terrible ever happened."

One of the gentlemen smirked at Cy. "How terrible can it be? You're a richer man now because of Edgar."

"As long as Enkidu is alive," Cy said, eyeballing me with an icy glare as if knowing full well that the two of us were tethered now just as Edgar and I were once joined.

Cy hated me. Loathed me. Despised me. That much was certain. However, I couldn't help but dread the moment when he would inevitably discover the truth about his beloved Edgar and me—the reality that there was something more between us, something that no one could ever possibly begin to understand.

After the gentlemen with leather briefcases and expensive-looking jewelry abandoned the house, the moment I had been dreading finally arrived: I was left alone with Cy.

I knew there was every possibility that he would ignore me, that he would continue to keep me locked away in the gated outdoor enclosure even on such an unusually humid summer evening. But then, something remarkable happened.

Cy appeared as if out of thin air, lurking beneath the vine-draped portico arranged beside the house's veranda. He stood there for a moment, gazing at me with such visible hatred, such unreserved animosity. As he idled there, I couldn't help but notice how he held a small notebook in his hands. I squinted and recognized the notebook as the same one Edgar would always write in late at night while we lounged in bed together.

Slowly, Cy approached my enclosure.

"You monster," he hissed at me, his brow furrowing and the corners of his lips curling. "If I could, I'd rip you limb from limb until you were confetti."

I straightened a little from my slumber, bleary-eyed at first. As Cy approached the locked gate, I could see his lips practically frothing with rage. He resembled one of the silverback gorillas I had seen at the zoo when I was much younger.

"How could you?" he asked.

But before I could make a movement—before I could do anything—Cy retreated to the house and disappeared through the double-paned glass doors, slamming them shut and nearly shattering them.

It was then that I knew. Cy had discovered the love Edgar and I shared when he wasn't present. Somehow, Cy had uncovered the truth. Perhaps Edgar had written about our romantic activities in his notebook. Perhaps Edgar had summarized in detail the physicality of our romance—the ways in which our bodies were joined in unbridled passion. I couldn't be certain how Cy had discovered the reality of our love, but there it was—finally out in the open.

There wasn't much I could do except to wait for Cy to return. I wondered if he would. I paced the enclosure for an hour or so and then when I was feeling especially sleepy, I crawled onto the small blanket they had arranged for me and began to doze off again.

I slept for mere minutes before I was awakened by the pitter-patter of what felt like raindrops pelting me in tiny beads. My eyelids fluttered open and my nostrils flexed at the acrid smell. It wasn't rain.

I glanced upward and saw Cy towering above me, his jeans unzipped and his genitals sprouting through the small opening where his legs met. He held himself with such confidence as he sprinkled me with his warm urine, lifting his manhood a little and aiming directly at my face as he continued to spray. I shifted away from him, dodging some of his seemingly unending geyser. But he shadowed me closely, straining with more urgency as the stream pelted me like an unarmed fire hose.

When he was finished, he zipped his pants up and staggered away from the enclosure like a toddler that had just learned how to walk for the first time. He glanced back at me in his drunken stupor and tossed an empty beer bottle at the only palm tree in my pen. It shattered, sparkling bits of glass scattering across the empty area as if they were discarded gemstones. Without uttering a single word, Cy stumbled into the house and disappeared from my sight once more.

I sat there for a moment, soaked and stinking with urine, and I wondered what I could do—what I could possibly do to get back at him, to make him understand the misery, the suffering, the agony I'd endured thanks to his cruelty.

It was then that I made the depressing realization of what I had to do if I wanted to escape Cy's vengeance for the love I shared with Edgar. I had to leave this place.

The next day, Cy didn't visit me much in my enclosure. Of course, I anticipated him to be present as soon as I woke up, looming above me and perhaps showering me once more. But he wasn't there.

I expected to see him eventually at my morning feeding, but he never showed. I began to worry: *What if he's going to leave me here? What if he's abandoned me already as well?*

I thought of scaling the fence and climbing my way to freedom, but the tips of each parapet circling the enclosure were outfitted with various spikes. It always bewildered me.

It felt as if Edgar never trusted me in the first place. It was as if he wanted me to remain in his care—or captivity if you really want to call it what it was—under his terms, under his conditions.

Even though it was a wasted thought, I considered what I might do if I was ever able to scale the fence and make my way into the forest just beyond the house. Perhaps there I would find a home, a refuge, a place where I might find love and affection once more. But it was a pointless thought. There was no way I'd be able to escape unless I could sneak out the main gateway the next time Cy arrived to deliver a meal. If he ever would again, that is.

Surely, he can't leave me here all alone, I thought to myself. *I'll starve.*

But perhaps that's exactly what he wanted. Perhaps his last cruelty was to leave me to die.

Thankfully, I wasn't left wondering for long as Cy appeared on the veranda later in the afternoon. He was dressed in one of Edgar's specially monogrammed red velvet robes that Edgar would often wear after the two of us had finished our lovemaking. I squinted at him, wondering why he was empty handed when he usually appeared at this time with a tray of food.

As he approached the enclosure, I began to skirt toward the main gateway where he was heading. I thought that if I was quick enough, I might be able to lurch past him while he opened the gate. Once I was outside the pen, it was only a couple hundred yards to the nearby forest's edge. Even if Cy did attempt to corral me once I finally escaped, there was every reasonable possibility that he wouldn't be quick enough.

Finally, Cy was standing at the gate and peering down at me.

"Back up, you little shit," he shouted at me.

But I wouldn't budge. I wouldn't move and instead I began clinging to the metal bars, incessantly drumming my hands against them as if insisting that he open the gate as swiftly as possible.

I watched as he dragged a set of keys from his pocket and pushed one of them into the lock, twisting it and gently leaning against the gate as it creaked open. Just as I was about to weave between Cy's legs and make a dash for the near tree line, I felt a swift kick in the center of my chest. I was on my back in a matter of seconds, bright lights shining in the corners of my vision. I slowly lifted myself up and it was then I realized that Cy had kicked me back further into the enclosure as I had landed near the outer rim of the small pool in the center of the space.

I straightened, leaning forward and watched as Cy entered the pen and locked the gate behind him. There it was. My first chance of escape—gone forever. Now I had only one more opportunity to get away: when he would eventually leave the enclosure. I knew it would be difficult. I understood that he would do everything in his power to keep me here, to keep me as a victim of his cruelty.

I felt myself wince a little as I watched him approach me. I shook my head in disbelief at his unusual smell. Cy always smelled so clean, so thoroughly washed. Today, for some inexplicable reason, he reeked like spoiled garbage.

"I always knew he loved you," Cy told me. "I guess I just never realized how much he cared about you. How deep it really was between the two of you."

Just then, Cy pulled a kitchen knife from his robe pocket. He brandished it in front of me, tilting the blade at me as it glistened in the sunlight.

"I've thought about this for a while," he said. "I think it's for the best. Edgar would want it this way."

Before I could react, before I could shriek at him or crawl

away to hide, Cy slashed at me and slid the knife into my shoulder. I hollered at the top of my lungs as he pulled the knife out of me. For a moment, my body heated, and it felt as though my every extremity had been launched into an incinerator. But then, just as suddenly, everything started to cool and the whole world around me began to blur.

I staggered away from Cy, clutching my shoulder as more blood soaked into my fur. But he was relentless. He followed me with the knife raised high. Finally, the moment had come we couldn't avoid anymore—one of us would not be leaving this enclosure alive.

Just as he was about to slash at me again, I lunged at his exposed arm and bit down hard. Cy screamed, the knife slipping from his hands and skating across the tiled pathway until it finally landed in the shallower end of the pool. Now that he was disarmed, he was exactly where I wanted him. I bit down again. This time, harder. I savored the metal taste of his blood, the tang of his exquisite agony. For once, I felt as if I were his superior, as if I were his lord and master and he were nothing more than a lowly servant. After all, I never wanted to be Cy's equal. I never wanted him to love me the way that my beloved Edgar had loved me and cared for me.

As Cy screamed, cradling his wounded arm and fountaining blood all over the freshly cleaned walkway, I lunged for his face and clawed at his eyes until I ripped them from their sockets.

Cy wobbled dizzily for a moment and then eventually slumped forward on the ground where I could get a better grasp on him. I heard him suffocating on wet, gurgling noises in the pit of his throat. He twitched there for what felt like hours, convulsing like a drowned insect. When it was finally all over, a dark ribbon of blood stretched from his body toward the rim of the nearby pool and dyed the clear water red.

Eric LaRocca

I sat there for a moment—mindlessly poking at his corpse, making certain he had perished and that there wasn't an ounce of life remaining in him. My opportunity to escape had passed. It was out of the question now. But perhaps that wasn't what I wanted, after all. Perhaps this is what I yearned for, what I longed for—to be a master to a man.

Days passed and nobody visited the house. I paced the enclosure, tediously going back and forth in front of the gate and praying someone might appear on the steps of the veranda and realize that I was still here. Of course, I wondered what they might do to me when they discovered what I had done to Cy. But I couldn't be bothered with that now. I was far too famished.

After a week or so, Cy's body had rotted significantly as it reclined under the bleeding yolk of the summer sun. It wasn't long before I decided that I should start eating parts of him since I knew that nobody else would arrive with fresh food. I went for the tenderest areas first—his armpits, his groin, his face. I took no pleasure in working the rubbery gristle from the white of his bone. In fact, I detested myself for what I had done to his body—how I had ravaged him, defiled him.

In a morbid way, I had been with Cy the same way that I had been with my dear Edgar.

To excuse myself from the guilt of having plundered him for meat, I took late afternoon laps in the pool. There were no thoughts of guilt following me while I floated on the water's surface. I was carefree, completely without concern as I bobbed there, and the water gently rocked me. From time to time, I imagined I was reclining in the arms of Edgar before the coppery scent of blood, the stench of rot reminded me of Cy, and it was never long before I was delivered to the present.

Still, for a few brief moments, I was delighted to forget everything—to find absolution in the calmness of water, in the sacred communion of an enemy's blood.

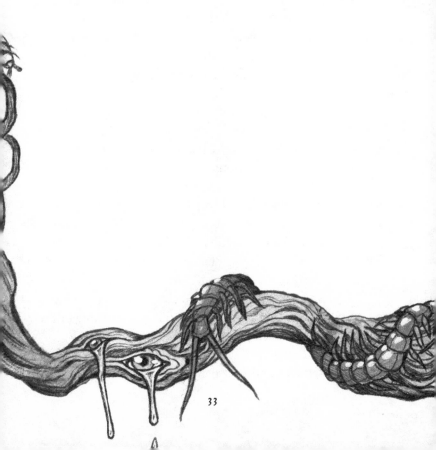

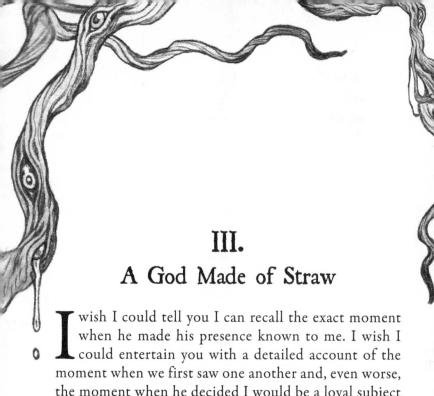

III.
A God Made of Straw

I wish I could tell you I can recall the exact moment when he made his presence known to me. I wish I could entertain you with a detailed account of the moment when we first saw one another and, even worse, the moment when he decided I would be a loyal subject to his each and every cruelty.

Sadly, no such meticulously detailed account exists in my memory. In fact, I can barely recall the first few days he came to visit the small nest I had managed to build in the crook of a scarecrow's shoulder. It's peculiar that I cannot summon a proper first impression of him—the small child dressed in dark overalls and wearing thick, round spectacles who always seemed so melancholy, so unbearably forlorn and lonely. I think it's most peculiar simply because nobody else has affected my life so considerably in the time I've endured as a living thing.

There was nothing exceptional about him. I'm sure you expect me to tell you that he was decidedly one thing or the other. But I'm afraid he wasn't.

Smaller children have always fascinated me—their playfulness, their inquisitive nature, their courage to explore.

The thing I can remember most about him is his despondency, his utter sadness as if he were carrying the weight of an unearned, invisible burden on his shoulders. I wonder if I've somehow managed to erase some of my memories of him in order to cope with the cruelties. I wonder if I've blotted out some of the more unsavory recollections to survive his mercilessness. Of course, I can't be certain; however, it makes little to no sense that I would not distinctly recall the person who changed my world forever.

I don't yearn to make the whole thing sound so dramatic, so excruciatingly theatrical. However, not much else has upended my world, my existence, my being more than the hatred and viciousness of a small child.

I recall watching him appear at the crest of the small hill in the distance about a hundred or so yards from the apron of tall grass. He's carrying a small stick he probably recovered from the nearby thicket and he's swatting at the gnats and horseflies circling his head. I watch him as he begins to weave through the field of corn, slashing at cornstalks with his stick as he passes through like a Puritan settler. When he's finally a few yards from where I'm perched on the scarecrow's shoulder, I make the decision to abandon the nest and roost in a nearby tree.

The little boy circles the scarecrow, pretending to challenge the straw-filled effigy to a duel as he slashes and stabs at him with the small stick. Then, he does exactly what I expect him to do—he climbs onto the figure and scampers up the pole until he's gripping the scarecrow's shoulder. Once there, he's able to peer inside the small nest I've built. I watch him carefully as his eyes covet the four black-speckled eggs I've arranged inside the nest. I think to swoop down at him from the branch where I've perched for the moment, but it's far too risky and I quietly curse myself for not being brave enough to stop him.

Even if I could have summoned the spirit to fly at him and chase him away, I would never have been able to prevent him from stealing one of my eggs. I watch him as he picks up one of the eggs, admiring it as he cups it in his palm.

I can't stop him, I think to myself. *No matter what I try to do, I can't prevent this from happening.*

Just then, he squeezes the small egg tight inside his fist. I sense my stomach curl at the horrible sight. I watch him as he opens his hand and regards the broken gooey bits of eggshell smeared against his skin like ivory specks of shredded paper. He laughs a little, as if genuinely amused by his cruelty— pleasantly charmed by his viciousness, his atrocity. Then, he scampers down from the scarecrow and begins to meander back through the maze of cornstalks until he reaches the grassy knoll in the distance.

Once he disappears beyond the hill and vanishes from sight, I dive down toward the nest and find the gooey remnants of what was once to be my child smeared across the scarecrow's vest and pants like glue.

I take a moment to mourn the loss, but before I'm lost and unfettered in a sea of misery and woe, I circle my nest on the scarecrow's shoulder and peer inside. There, I find three remaining eggs—my sweet and precious ones. For some reason, he left them. I quietly thank God for little mercies such as that.

I nestle myself there, blanketing the eggs with my body. For a brief moment, I feel lost—uncertain what to do, fearful he might return soon with a desire to crush the other eggs and successfully obliterate any chance I have to become a mother.

Out of my peripheral vision, I notice the scarecrow leering at me—his shiny, black buttons for eyes, his pencil-thin lips drawn in permanent marker on a burlap sack filled with straw.

In a moment of weakness, I pray to him:
Please don't let him come back. Please keep us safe.

The wind whispers all around me, as if it were the voice of an immortal deity—as if he were telling me that he would protect me and my children no matter what.

For weeks, there's no sign of the child. He doesn't visit as regularly as he used to and I'm, of course, I'm more than grateful for his absence.

It isn't long before the three remaining eggs finally hatch and the nest is filled with precious babies, their small mouths constantly opening and blindly searching the air for food.

I do my best to hunt in the nearby tall grass for worms and other insects to bring to the nest for my offspring. I've come to terms with the fact that I would do anything for them. I know for certain I was fearful before and unable to stop the boy from squeezing the egg, but I realize I must never allow something like that to happen ever again.

In fact, perhaps it won't, I think to myself.

After all, it's been weeks since I've seen the child and there's a good possibility he might not return.

Of course, I'm immediately regretful of being so optimistic when one afternoon, I notice a small figure dressed in a red shirt and blue shorts meandering along the narrow causeway leading toward the field of corn. He's empty handed this time and I'm momentarily grateful he hasn't arrived with a stick or any other weapon for that matter. Then again, what would it matter? The last time he was here, he used his hands quite skillfully and could do the same again without reservation.

As he drifts through the tide of cornstalks, I reluctantly

take my leave and relocate to the same nearby tree branch where I had perched the last time. I loathe myself for my cowardice, but what else could I do? The babies are much too young to fly and I certainly can't bring them with me. I figure I'll wait a few moments before I'll make a hasty decision on what should be done about the little monster.

Finally, the moment arrives that I had been dreading: the little boy arrives in the small clearing where the scarecrow is arranged. This time, however, the boy does not hesitate. He grabs hold of the straw figure's leg and hoists himself up until he's eye level with the nest perched on the scarecrow's shoulder. He peers over the rim of the nest and sees my babies nestled inside the small bowl of twigs and dirt I've built there.

For a moment, he merely gazes at them with wonderment—the wonderment of an explorer who has just witnessed something truly remarkable, something extraordinarily grand. However, his enchantment does not linger for long. I watch him as he reaches into his pocket and pulls out a small toothpick, admiring it as if he were about to make good use of it. He proves me right. Without warning, he shoves the toothpick inside one of my babies and spears its little wing. The baby bird trembles, impaled. I can hear its brittle shrieks as it calls out for me.

I'm paralyzed. I cannot move. I merely linger on the branch and watch in horror as the little boy pries open the small beak of another baby bird and shoves a toothpick down its throat. Finally, he comes upon the last remaining baby bird in the nest and skewers its head with a final toothpick.

When he's satisfied with his handiwork, he admires the abomination he's conjured—a grotesque tableau of carnage and suffering at the expense of my little ones. The thing that perplexes me so terribly is that he killed them with such ease, such effortlessness as if he were ordered by a superior to complete the task—as if he were a mere servant to a merciless and unforgiving god.

I watch him as he begins to scamper down the scarecrow, abandoning his ugly creation almost as suddenly as he had built it. Just then, I notice him losing his balance. He teeters a little, swiping at the scarecrow's arm to hold him upright. But, for a moment, it almost looks as though the scarecrow is pushing him away, banishing him from the sanctity of his domain.

It can't be, though, I think to myself. *Could the thing have come to life to help me?*

The little boy cries out, and for once he looks indisputably scared. His genuine fear does little to save him, however. He swipes at the scarecrow's sleeve once more and pulls out a clump of wet straw just before he plummets to the ground, his head slamming against a large rock with an obscene thud. I watch his limbs twitch for moment, blood like maple syrup creeping from underneath his dark hair. Finally, he's without movement.

I can tell he's dead.

I don't hesitate. I swoop down toward the nest and find my precious little ones speared and gouged, their tiny corpses huddled together as if begging to find a modicum of tenderness and care in their final moments.

When I'm finished grieving for the babies I hardly had the chance to care for, I make my way toward the edge of the nest and peer down at the little boy's body splayed out at the foot of the massive scarecrow. Naturally, I wonder what possessed his cruelty, what made him seek me out to persecute and torture. It pains me when I realize I'll never know.

I sail back up to the ledge on the scarecrow's shoulder

where I've built my nest. There's a part of me that desperately wants to thank the straw-filled effigy even if it can't respond. I wonder what it might say if it could. I wonder if it might lovingly cradle me, if it might promise me that it would do more to protect me and my babies next time.

Just as I'm about to fly away, a black glove filled with bits of straw gently pats me on the head.

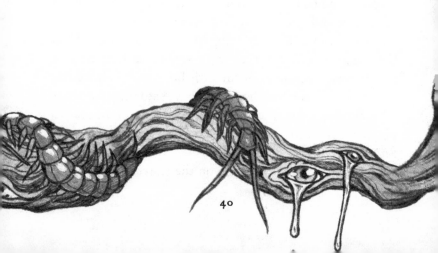

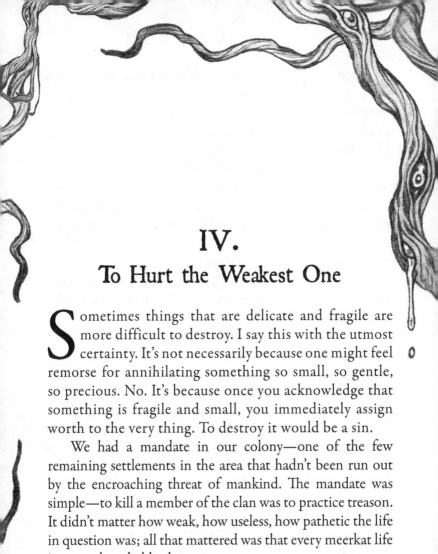

IV.
To Hurt the Weakest One

Sometimes things that are delicate and fragile are more difficult to destroy. I say this with the utmost certainty. It's not necessarily because one might feel remorse for annihilating something so small, so gentle, so precious. No. It's because once you acknowledge that something is fragile and small, you immediately assign worth to the very thing. To destroy it would be a sin.

We had a mandate in our colony—one of the few remaining settlements in the area that hadn't been run out by the encroaching threat of mankind. The mandate was simple—to kill a member of the clan was to practice treason. It didn't matter how weak, how useless, how pathetic the life in question was; all that mattered was that every meerkat life in our colony held value.

It made little sense to me, considering the fact that I had come up in another colony of meerkats that were especially ruthless. I was one of the few that survived and my mother constantly reminded me of my strength, my determination, my resolve to endure despite the way in which the world wants to obliterate things that are small and feeble. I wasn't feeble for long, thankfully. It wasn't much time before we

migrated, and I soon found myself mated with an especially virile male from a neighboring colony. Our litter of pups were born not long after we had mated and one of the leaders of our clan congratulated me on such a glorious abundance of healthy babies. That is, except for one.

I knew there was something queer about him from the moment I first smelled him. There's a particular stench when it comes to meerkat fragility—an overpowering aroma that nearly stopped me dead in my tracks whenever I inhaled his scent. I mentioned to my mate how it might be preferable to not name this particular pup just in case nature takes its cruel course. But the clan insisted that we name him, and I was once again reminded that all lives in the colony have worth.

So, we named him Tol.

He was much smaller than the other pups and seemed to stop growing after a few weeks. Even worse, the other pups would intentionally leave him out and trample over him if he was in their way.

I neither despised Tol nor hated his shortcomings, but I would be lying if I didn't tell you that his inadequacies caused me to worry that he might somehow undo the integrity and safety of our colony. After all, the leaders of our pack had intentions of migrating west to another burrow in a week or so to avoid some of the rain. I knew Tol wouldn't be able to make the journey. I knew that he would always have restrictions and, therefore, those limitations would be a detriment to us.

My mate, Pasco, never seemed to worry. Even when I approached him about the upcoming migration west and when I expressed how I was worried that Tol might prevent us from making the journey with the rest of the clan.

"You can stay with him," Pasco said to me. "I'll go with the rest of the pups, and you can stay behind with Tol if he can't manage to keep up."

I flashed him a look of bewilderment at his suggestion.

"Isn't that what a mother is supposed to do?" he asked, bewildered.

Remembering my lower station, I merely nodded and kept my head lowered. But what I didn't tell him was that I didn't want to be Tol's mother. I loathed the idea of playing the role of mother to something so weak, so helpless. I didn't want to be left all alone with the sickly pup I couldn't even stand to smell. I was afraid he would need me in such a way that I could not provide, that I could not properly comfort him or even care to comfort him. I did not love him. I did not care for him the same way I cared for my other pups. This was evident in the way I quickened my pace when I noticed he was lagging behind the rest of the pups, and it was especially apparent when I purposefully pushed food out of his way so that the others could eat.

"Do you want him to stay a runt forever?" Pasco asked me, noticing how I seemed to dote on the others and abandon Tol with such urgency. "He'll never grow if he goes wanting for your love."

That was the problem. Tol would never have my love. He was a nuisance, a burden—a liability that would weigh us down and prevent us from thriving with the other meerkats in the colony. Perhaps Pasco didn't feel this way. Fathers are decidedly removed from their pups, after all. It always comes back to the mother's responsibility. Tol would remain under my care and would continue to be a drain on me until he either grew and could fend for himself or until he inevitably perished.

Finally, the day arrived that I had been dreading—the great migration west. We began our journey in the early morning. For a while, things went smoothly. Tol kept up with the rest of the colony despite the slowness of his pace.

Eric LaRocca

However, it wasn't long before I noticed the journey began to tax him more than the others. I noticed how he had slowed to a crawl, constantly lagging behind the rest of the group and begging me to stay with him so that he wouldn't be left alone.

"You'll have to do better than that," I told him. "They're expecting us to keep up with the group."

Tol wheezed, barely about to breathe. "You promise you'll stay with me—?"

I despised him for asking me to promise him something so loathsome. I didn't want to be tethered to him. But I was. I would be for as long as he was alive.

"You're going to have to stay with him," Pasco told me as he herded the rest of our pups. "You'll catch up eventually and we'll all meet together at the new burrow."

It wasn't a question. It was a demand from him. Who was I to question my mate?

It was when we watched the rest of the colony move ahead, their shapes thinning to mere specks on the horizon that I began to think truly reprehensible thoughts. For the first time in my life, I began to entertain exceptionally shameful thoughts. I thought of leaving Tol there in the scorching desert sun to shrivel and crisp until blackened—a morsel to be plucked by one of the large black birds already circling us overhead. I knew that if I left him there, if I abandoned him, there was every possibility that his remains would be found by the others in the colony on our return trip. It would be wicked to be such a neglectful mother—to allow the vultures and other eaters of carrion to devour my weakest pup.

I was his mother.

If anyone was going to hurt him, it had to be me.

It was then that I made the decision that I would devour

him. I made the decision to smear him from the world—to obliterate him, to wipe him out until not even his shadow remained.

When we stopped to rest, I decided that I would do it then. I told him to find a cool place beneath one of the trees to doze for a bit while I hunted, and he agreed without comment. For a moment, I watched him as he settled himself and found a quiet spot to nest for a bit. He looked so small, so weak, so fragile. I knew this would be difficult. After all, things that are fragile are so difficult to hurt. I knew this well.

When I was certain he was sleeping, I crept upon him and regarded him for what felt like hours. I watch him as he stirred gently, his legs twitching while sleep claimed him. I knew there would be no turning back if I decided to do this. I knew I would have to eat him and eat him entirely so that his remains would not be found.

Before another moment of hesitation, I clamped down on his neck and seized him. His eyelids fluttered opened for a moment and he looked at me with such confusion. His bewilderment did not last long because I snapped his neck not long after. One swift motion and the deed was done. It broke with a vulgar crunching sound. Tol dangled there, lifeless, in my grasp. It felt peculiar to hold him—to cradle him as if he were once again a newborn with so much potential, so much spirit residing within him.

I knew if I considered it for too long, I would become maudlin. I didn't want that. I wanted to catch up with the rest of the colony and pretend Tol had never even existed in the first place.

I knew that before I could do that, I would have to feed.

After I finished devouring Tol, there was nothing but bits of bones left from him—a shining sculpture puzzle of his anatomy, the very last few artifacts from a life that should have never existed. I dug a hole near the base of a nearby tree and buried him there.

Just as I was about to search for a watering hole to wash some of the blood from my fur, Pasco surprised me. He was leering at me, crawling toward the grave I had dug for our pup.

"What have you done?" he asked me, his eyes wide and fearful of the answer.

I noticed him studying with such intent the bits of blood matted into my fur in thick knots. There was his answer—dripping from my snout and soaking my paws.

I hesitated to answer him. When I was finally able to push the words out, I noticed other members of the colony appearing behind him. They, too, searched me with wide, cautious eyes—visibly fearful of such a grotesque sight.

"What are you all doing here?" I asked Pasco.

He looked surprised I would even ask, as if silently telling me that I had no right to be so incredulous, so suspicious. "We came back for you both."

His words hung in the air like a dim vapor. I could tell that he knew there was nothing left of Tol. Our pup was gone. I had eaten him and buried him deep so that ruthless scavengers wouldn't dig up his bones.

I knew what they would do to me. I knew the punishment for hurting one of our pack members—for destroying something so precious, so dear. They would either snap my neck like I had done to Tol and feast on my remains or, worse, they would abandon me to fend for myself.

Pasco approached me after he had a few words with one of the pack leaders. I knew what he was going to tell me. I knew for certain it wasn't going to be pleasant news.

He winced when he told me what they were going to do to me—how they were planning to punish me. He winced because even a guilt-faced pup murderer like me is difficult to hurt, to inflict pain upon with such reckless abandon. I could tell it pained him to know the details of how they were going to make me suffer.

But he knew it had to be done. How could I possibly fault him for that?

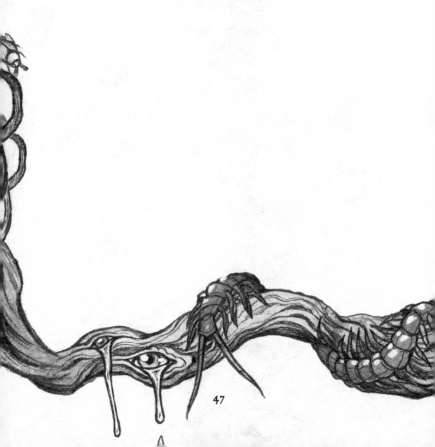

Bird and Bug are Happy

"**D**o I...have to say my name?" the young girl asks her over the phone.

Bug senses her face soften. Her voice gentle, lips touching the mouthpiece as she speaks to her. "No. You don't have to tell me anything you don't want to."

The girl's voice shudders with relief, whimpering. "OK. Thanks."

"Can you tell me how old you are?" Bug asks, leaning forward in her chair.

"Eighteen."

Bug makes a note on the small pad of paper on her desk. "OK."

The girl chokes on quiet sobs, the words clogging her throat. "Sometimes—I cut myself."

"Do you have anything near you right now that could be used to hurt you?"

"There's a razor in the bathroom," the girl says.

"And where are you now?"

"My bedroom," she answers.

Although this response is preferable, Bug still isn't

comforted. After all, she knows full well that any room with a bed in it is a place where a young woman can be hurt.

"Can you promise me you'll stay where you are while you're on the phone with me?" Bug asks her.

The girl whimpers like a small animal caught in a trap. "Yeah."

"OK," Bug says. "That's good to hear."

Bug thinks of herself when she was eighteen. She thinks of how there's an invisible expiration date stamped on the forehead of every queer person—how most of society, even other queer people, expect you to wither away, to languish in torment and eventually expire from some incurable illness as if it were proper contrition for your perversity. She thinks of how unusual it must be for the neighbors to suffer in her presence—a sixty-seven-year-old dyke with an uncorrected overbite and a touch of fibromyalgia.

She can't help but wonder if her wife feels the same way—if somehow her wife senses the same eagerness from others to eventually go extinct so that you're less of a public nuisance, less of a reminder that queer people do, in fact, share the same suffering as the rest of humanity.

Bug thinks of asking her wife that when she comes upon her in the kitchen, but Bird looks so cheerful while preparing dinner. She can hardly bring herself to say anything as she regards her beloved. After all, everything seems more pleasant when Bird is near. Bug glances around the kitchen, reminded of the paintings Bird had completed over the years. Her favorite subject—Bug as the statue of the Venus de Milo. There's a sadness when Bug looks at them now, however—Bird's once confident and assured brush strokes have weakened considerably, and the newer paintings are now crude imitations of art that not even a child would be honored to call their own.

Bug glances at the kitchen table and senses her face drain of color when she notices how the plates and silverware have been arranged upside down.

"Almost ready," Bird tells her, flitting from the refrigerator to the kitchen counter. "Always smells better when you cook, though."

Bug goes to the stove and grimaces, finding the oven cold.

"The oven's not on."

Bird turns, bewildered. Her voice thins.

"No—?"

Bug opens the oven door and touches the cold breast of chicken.

"It's still cold, Bird," she says.

Bird stands still, face wrinkling with dismay.

"I—I thought I—"

But she can't finish the sentence.

Bug guides Bird to a chair at the kitchen table. "Here. You sit down and relax. I'll heat up something."

She notices how Bird begins to sulk like a scolded child with her arms crossed and her brow furrowed.

"I wanted it ready for you, Bug."

Bug kneels in front of her, turning her face to hers.

"Hey. How does it go?"

Bird does not respond.

"You know. How does it go? Bird eats Bug—"

Bird draws a heavy breath, closing her eyes as if preparing for something.

"Bug feeds Bird," she says.

Bug leans a little closer, petting Bird's wrinkled hand. "Bird and Bug—"

"—are happy."

Bug smiles, pecking Bird's forehead with a kiss.

Then, she goes to the refrigerator and begins rummaging through the pile of half-empty leftover containers.

"But it should've been ready for you," Bird insists, staring at the floor.

"I know. It's OK."

"The timer must be broken," Bird says, shaking her head. "I'll have to take a look at it tomorrow."

Bug pulls out a container of juice and a pitcher of water from the refrigerator. "Juice or water?"

But Bird does not answer. She sits there, motionless. Her eyes—dimmed and glasslike.

"Bird?"

As Bug approaches her, Bird stirs in her chair as if waking from a dream. She shouts her rehearsed speech with fervor as if reciting a Shakespearean soliloquy.

"With her left hand, the Venus cradled the apple given to her by Paris and with her right held up the cloth draped about her waist," she says. "Her gaze returned to the apple, and she reflected on the magnificence of her victory."

Bug senses a look of dread passing over her face. She closes the refrigerator door and gently approaches her wife.

Bird's mouth opens with soundless words, her eyes lowering and body stiffening.

"Bird," Bug quietly says. "You go to see Dr. Parson on Wednesday?"

Bird's eyes suddenly widen. Dread.

"I forgot something," she says.

She rises from her seat mechanically.

"Bird?"

Bird hastens to the small bathroom adjoining the kitchen and bends down in front of the cat's litter box.

Bug rushes after her and finds her bent over to the box, her eyes inspecting every corner of the receptacle.

"Bird, it can wait," she tells her.

But Bird can't be persuaded. Bird grabs both sides of

the container and shakes it back and forth. She pauses for moment, as if waiting for something—as if she were a swami and reading tea leaves in the bottom of an empty cup.

"Bird, please," Bug begs her wife.

Just then, Bird reaches inside the litter box and begins rearranging the wet clumps of urine and feces with her hands. Bug grabs her arm, shouting at her.

"Bird, no. Don't touch that."

"But it's not clean yet," Bird tells her, hands trembling.

"We don't clean it like that. We use the plastic bags."

Bug takes her wife's hands and leads her to the small sink. She turns on the faucet and runs her hands beneath the warm water.

"You'll get sick," she tells her as she lathers Bird's hands with soap, scrubbing them.

"I'm not sick," Bird insists.

"I know."

Bird glances back at the litter box, her eyes filled with sorrow and longing. "I didn't finish cleaning it."

"I'll take care of it. OK?"

Bug turns off the hot water.

Bird stares at both of her freshly cleaned hands. She recites with a nervous, rehearsed conviction: "Date: 101 BC. Media: Marble. Height: Six feet, three inches. Subject: Venus."

She repeats this again and again, her voice thinning to a mere whisper as she goes over each and every word.

"You sit and relax," Bug tells her.

Bird ambles toward the kitchen table and sits, eyes never leaving her hands. She repeats her recitation again and again until finally Bug kneels in front of her and takes both Bird's hands in hers.

"Bird," she whispers.

Bird's voice quiets. Her lips continue to move with silent words as she regards her wife.

"Thank you for helping me," Bug says.

Bird's hands stop fidgeting. Her entire body quiets.

"I was just—trying to remember."

Bug begins rearranging the improperly placed silverware and plates on the kitchen table.

"You see Dr. Parson on Wednesday?" Bug asks.

Bird merely nods.

"I'll drive you," Bug says.

"No."

"I want to."

Bird shakes her head. "So you can hold my hand?"

Bug recoils, hurt a little. "You don't want me to come?"

"I'll go on my own."

"I'm happy to come," Bug says.

Bird rolls her eyes. "I know you are."

"I just thought it might be best if I come too," Bug says, hopeful she might accept without resistance.

Bird's tone firms. "I won't be long."

"I'm driving you, Bird," Bug says.

Bird glares at Bug with a visible accusation. "Where are my keys?"

Bug chooses to ignore her. "I can heat up that leg of lamb we didn't finish last night."

"Where are they, Bug?"

Bug's eyes avoid Bird at all costs. "I'll hold on to them."

Bird rises from her chair, her lips curling. "Where are they?"

"What do we say?" Bug asks. "Bird eats Bug—"

"What did you do with them?"

"Bird eats Bug. Finish it."

"I want my keys," Bird shouts.

Bug opens a container of leftover food on the counter and empties some onto a nearby plate. "Dr. Parson and I don't want you hurting yourself. He's already mentioned we start considering other options."

Bug can't help but notice how Bird's eyes begin to cramp with dread.

"Other options?" Bird asks.

Bug doesn't want to say it. She hadn't planned to ever reveal to Bird what she and her doctor had discussed. But with every passing day Bird seemed to deteriorate more and more quickly. Bug couldn't help but wonder if she would ever get better. She knew those with Bird's diagnosis never did.

"The Pines," she says quietly.

Bird shrinks from her. "You could do that to me?"

Bug glances at Bird and notices how her wife's face begins to droop, her eyes filling with dread like an elderly dog that has just seen its owner carrying a rifle.

"You know what that place is, Bug," she says.

"I don't want you to leave," Bug says. "I want to take care of you. Haven't I always?"

Bird's eyes light up, sparkling. "I know what this is about."

"I'm only taking the keys away to help you."

"The letter," Bird says.

Bug turns, her mouth hanging open.

"What?"

"You read it."

"What letter?" Bug asks.

"How did you find it?"

"Bird."

"At least she still cares," Bird says.

Bug doesn't want to ask. "Who?"

"Who do you think?"

Bug senses the warmth leave her cheeks. She feels

something as hot as iron settle, curling in the pit of her stomach. She knows exactly to whom Bird is referring.

"She—sent you a letter?"

"I thought you read it," Bird says.

Bug shakes her head in disbelief. "Why did she send you a letter?"

"She must've hand delivered it."

"Where is it?"

Bird looks off, distant and dreaming. "I knew she would. Violet was always thoughtful that way."

Bug's hands curl into fists. "Don't—say her name."

"At least she still cares," Bird says.

"Let me read it."

"You can't," Bird explains.

"I want to."

"I already burned it."

Bird then storms out of the kitchen, darting into the library.

Bug inhales nervously.

She starts to follow Bird, but stops. One of Bird's framed paintings on the wall hangs there, crooked. She straightens it, for a moment admiring the artwork—one of Bird's earlier pieces when her artistic prowess wasn't a question. She studies the painted figure of the limbless Goddess—chiffon draped about her waist, nipples stiffened, and a distant, far-off look in her eyes. Bug remembers exactly what she was thinking when she modeled for this painting. She recalls how she had once thought: "This is the happiest I'll ever be." She's devastated to know now that she was right.

After adjusting the painting on the wall, she skirts into the library and finds Bird in the corner of the room where the bookshelves meet. She's furiously scrubbing a statuette of the Venus de Milo with a small toothbrush.

"You weren't going to tell me?" Bug asks her.

As Bird sets the statuette down, she notices how the shelf begins to tilt slightly. She lovingly removes the statuette and begins to fiddle with the teetering shelf.

"Tell you?" Bird asks.

"About the letter."

"I didn't want to upset you."

Bug sprints over toward the desk and begins rummaging through each of the drawers crammed with sheets filled with half-finished sketches and makeshift drawings of various parts of human anatomy.

"Where is it?"

"I told you," Bird says. "I burned it."

"I don't believe you, Bird."

Bird shakes her head. "I shouldn't have told you."

"What did she say?"

"Nothing."

"You're lying."

"She just said she had thought of me," Bird explains. "Her dissertation on "Crocodile cults in Graeco-Roman Egypt" had finally been accepted."

"You'd still be teaching if it weren't for her," Bug says, folding her arms and pacing like a frightened animal.

"I didn't want to keep teaching, Bug."

"You would've still been respected by them."

"Those Neanderthals wouldn't know an early Picasso from a pierogi. Besides, a resignation is better than a dismissal."

The words well up in Bug's throat as it tightens. "I wouldn't have to drive two towns over just to buy milk and eggs."

"It's been eight years," Bird reminds her.

"I wish I could forget like you."

Bug realizes the obscenity of what she's said and covers her mouth, surprised at her own cruelty.

"I'm sorry," she says. "She ruined everything for us. Everything for you."

Bird approaches her, letting a hand rest on her shoulder. "Are you forgetting it was my fault too?"

"No. It was her."

"You think it wasn't me, too?"

"Don't say that."

"Say what?" Bird asks. "That I wanted it, too."

"Bird."

Bug winces, as if anticipating a more hurtful confession to come. Finally, Bird makes it:

"And that—sometimes—I want it still."

Without any warning, Bug swings her arm across the desk. Papers scatter everywhere in a flurry. The statuette of the Venus de Milo smashes on the floor.

Bug's face reddens with anger and embarrassment, and she hurries out of the room, a blast of warm air following her.

Bug stirs in bed, her eyes still closed.

She stretches both arms above her head, her whole body shuddering with the satisfaction of a night of rest.

Opening her eyes, Bug reaches out to touch Bird, but finds her gone and her side of the bed already dressed.

She chews her fingernails. Her eyes scan the empty room.

After taking a shower, Bug confronts the thing she loathes the most: her reflection in the bathroom mirror.

She stands there for a moment, a towel wrapped around her head of wet hair.

Bird and Bug are Happy

She dabs her fingers in the small container of lotion and smears some on her chin. It's then that her fingers recognize the looseness of skin running down her neck.

Bug gently tugs, her skin stretching like elastic. She frowns, teeth clenching as she continues to pull. Another yank and the flesh peels from her neck and highlights a supple, healthy pinkness beneath. Her new skin beneath, however, appears hard and shines as if it were plastic.

The rubbery pleat of old skin wiggles in Bug's hand. Her curiosity soon turns to concern, and she lets it slip from between her fingers.

Eyes returning to her reflection, her hands move over the newly exposed skin. Her fingers tour the roundness of a small, dark birthmark now fixed at the center of her throat.

It's not long, however, before her eyes locate another peculiarity.

She leans closer to the glass, her breath whistling.

She doesn't believe it.

She holds her eyelid open just to be sure.

One eye—its usual shade of dark brown.

The other—jade green.

Her mouth hangs open, as if desperately trying to comprehend.

A gust of wind murmurs around her, lifting her hair.

Bird, eyes guarded with goggles, hunches over her workbench. The circular saw revs as Bird guides a plank of wood beneath the spinning blade.

Bug glides down the cellar steps, scowling at the sight of Bird working near the saw.

"Bird. Turn it off," she demands.

Bird, startled, turns the saw off. The blade slows, screeching, until it's finally silent.

"The shelf needed to be fixed," Bird explains.

"I don't want you running that machine anymore."

"But I'm not finished," Bird says.

Bug gathers a dirty sheet left on the cellar floor and covers the table saw with it.

"I'll call and have the Feller's son take it away tomorrow," she says.

"You're not going to have anybody take it away."

"It's too dangerous," Bug says.

Bird crosses her arms, clearly exasperated with Bug already. "Is that all, Bug?"

Bug senses her face whiten.

"No," she says.

Bird turns away from Bug and back to the work laid out on her bench.

"I—wanted to say I was sorry."

Bug notices a small picture pinned to the side of Bird's workbench. It's a photo of them—much younger—with backpacks strapped to their shoulders, a smile on both of their faces, and a thick forest of greenery behind them.

"You still have this picture?"

"It's my favorite."

"Mine, too."

Bird takes off her goggles and throws a white sheet over her work bench.

"I'll call you if I'm late tonight," Bird says.

Bug does a double take, thinking she had misheard her. "Tonight?"

"Shouldn't take too long."

"You go to see Dr. Parson tomorrow. I'm driving you. Remember?"

"Not to the doctor's office. To campus," Bird explains. "I have a meeting with Violet at three about her thesis. I'm already late. Did I tell you she told me she had read my doctoral dissertation on the Venus de Milo? She even quoted it to me."

"Bird, you're confused," Bug says. "Here. Sit."

She moves a stool closer to her wife. But Bird resists.

"Violet's waiting for me."

Bug's voice firms.

"I told you I don't want to hear her name, Bird."

Bird looks closely at Bug, eyes narrowing.

"Who are you?" she asks.

"Bird?"

Bird begins to glance around the cellar, panicked. "Where's Bug?"

"I'm right here."

"You're—different."

"I'm not."

Bird, wide-eyed, still looks about.

"I don't think—You're not the same."

"No."

"You've changed," she says.

Bug takes her wife's hands.

"I haven't. I promise. Please believe me."

Bug's eyes water, tears beading in the corners of her eyes. She notices how her wife's face softens.

"See? It's me. It's Bug."

Bird stares at her, blankly. Her face relaxes, realizing only slightly.

She exhales: "Bug."

Bug wraps her arms around her, kissing her neck. If she could, she'd reach inside her and drag out the rotted weed of her memory and water it until it was healthy, pink, and new once more.

If only I could, she thinks to herself. *If only she could.*

Bird reclines on the bed, reading a book. The television plays in the background, a silver glow rinsing the wall.

Bug stands in front of the bedroom mirror, taking off her clothes. She looks at Bird, hoping she'll draw her attention from her book.

But she never looks up.

Bug turns her head back to her reflection, removing her shirt. Her hands move about her stomach, fingers following the lines of stretch marks running the length of her sagging midriff.

She frowns.

She looks at her eyes—both blue. She can't help but notice an apron of loose flesh hanging from her chin. She wets her hand and presses it down.

Bug takes a deep breath and slips on her pajamas.

She goes to her side of the bed and begins undressing the sheets. Looking at Bird, her mouth opens several times without words before she finally speaks.

"Bird—"

Bird makes a grunt of acknowledgement, her attention never leaving her book.

"What did you mean today when you said I was different? That I had—changed."

Bird looks at Bug queerly.

"Did I—?"

Bug doesn't want to ask. She does anyway:

"What did you mean?"

"Doesn't everything change?" Bird asks. "You were my model before you were my lover. Look how we changed."

"Did you mean the way I look—or the way I am?" Bug asks her.

Bird shakes her head. "I don't know."
"Had you been thinking it for a while?"

"What do you mean?"

Bug climbs into bed, pulling the sheets up around her. "You know. Was it something you just thought of today? Or have you thought I've been different for a while now?"

Bird thinks, the question troubling her.

"For a while. I guess."
"What do you mean?"
"It's all changed," Bird tells her. "You're not who I want you to be."
Bug's voice trembles. "To be what?"
Bird looks away, closing her book. "It's all different now."
"Since when?"
"When do you think?"
The word is Bug's only plea: "Bird."
"Venus," Bird gently says.
"You mean—Violet?"
"No. You were never as beautiful as she was. Still is."
Bird shakes her head, as if ashamed to even confess, "I could never love you the way I loved her."
Bug turns away from her wife, her eyes watering.
But suddenly, Bird touches her and pulls her back toward her until they're facing each other.
"What is it?" Bug asks, dabbing some of the wetness from her eyes.
"Your skin," Bird says. "It feels—different."
Bug deflates. "I know," she says. "There's something wrong with me."
Bird's fingers touch the loose fold of skin hanging from Bug's chin.

"It's strange," Bird says. "How people so close can eventually become strangers."

"Bird," Bug says gently. "I'm scared."

"What do we say?" Bird asks, pulling Bug a little closer. "Bird eats Bug."

Bug senses her breathing becoming more and more shallow as Bird's hands fiddle with the loose flap of skin hanging from her skin as if it were melted wax.

"Bug feeds Bird," Bug says.

Bug begins to whimper softly as Bird lifts the loose skirt of skin from Bug's chin.

"Bird and Bug—"

"—are happy."

And with that, Bird wrenches the entire mask of skin from Bug's face, highlighting the glistening red sinew of Bug's muscle.

Bug screams until she's hoarse, until the sound is muted by a violent hiss of wind, and she wakes up from the nightmare.

Bug shudders, her entire body springing up from sleep. Hair glued to her forehead with beads of sweat, she pants.

She looks about the empty bedroom.

Bug sees a statuette of the limbless Venus de Milo situated on the nightstand. She turns on her side, facing away from it. Pauses. She can't help herself. She jerks back and shoves it inside a drawer.

More ribbons of Bug's peeled flesh—loose transparent threads like discarded curls of snakeskin—are littered about the sheets. She pulls more from her throat and chin.

It's her hair that she now notices—the color red. She holds the strings of hair close to her face, mouth open in disbelief.

Bug throws off the sheets and rushes over to the bedroom's vanity. She switches on the lamp and leans in close to the glass, her breathing growing shallower.

Her fingers nervously run through the curls of red that now fall past her shoulders.

A gust of wind surrounds her.

Bug thinks she sees something else.

She does.

She leans into the glass again.

It's then that she sees the slope of her nose gently begin to shift upward and then back down. One of her eyes responds, violently stirring in its socket.

Bug covers her mouth, suffocating a scream.

She hastens into the bathroom where she finds Bird dressing. Bug sobs, leaning into her wife's arms. But Bird immediately pulls away, as if distrustful.

"Bird. Something's wrong."

Bird staggers away, easing into the corner of the room where the walls meet.

"Who are you?" she asks.

"I'm scared," Bug says.

"Where's my wife?"

"Bird, it's me. It's Bug."

Bird grabs a razor on the counter and swings at Bug, slicing her hand. Bug screams, vaulting back.

"Bird, no. It's me."

"Why are you in my house?" Bird asks, brandishing the razor as if preparing to make good use of it again.

"It's me. Bug."

But Bug sees the distrust residing in Bird's eyes. She notices how her wife glances at the open bathroom door—the only way out.

"I'm calling the police.

"No. It's Bug," she says, clutching her bleeding hand and whimpering. "What do we say? Bird feeds Bug."

"You're not her."

"Something's happening to me."

Bird swats at her with the razor again, screeching like frightened swine.

"Stay away from me," she shouts.

"Listen to me."

"You're not her."

"I am."

"You're not Venus."

"Bird. Please."

Once again, Bird slashes at her with the razor.

Bug falls back, screaming. She staggers out of the bathroom and down the hallway.

Bug, clutching her hand, hastens down the cellar steps and into Bird's workroom. Opera music drifts from the small stereo on Bird's workbench.

Eyes watering and breath shallow, Bug rushes over to the workbench and tears the photograph from the wall. She holds it in her hands, staring at it and blinking through her tears.

Her wounded hand pains her. She looks about the bench for cloth and dressings. Finding a small box of bandages, she tightly wraps her hand.

Her eyes scan the seemingly endless drawings and sketches of the Venus de Milo pinned on the cellar wall. She clears the wetness from both eyes.

Her reflection in a small mirror set out on the workbench catches her eye. She stares at herself. Her lips pulling down, her eyes are filled with hopelessness. Face hardening with anger, she smashes the mirror on the ground.

The shards of glass shatter on the floor, some bits skating beneath the table holding the sheet-dressed table saw. Bug slowly approaches the table.

The sound of Bird's voice echoes throughout the

corridors of her mind: *"It's strange. How people so close can become strangers."*

She lifts the sheet, uncovering the saw. The blade glistens in the light. It whispers to her.

A soft gust of wind blows past her.

She finds the cord running beneath the table and plugs it into an outlet fixed in the wall. Pressing a switch, the blade whirs alive, humming.

Bug circles the table, her eyes never leaving the spinning saw as it gently sings to her. After finding rope, she stretches her arm across the board and fastens her hand to the leg of the table.

Bird's voice circles in Bug's head like an angry current, as livid as whitewater: *"It's changed. You're not who I want you to be."*

Bug sobs, panting, as she begins to direct the table saw toward her outstretched arm.

She closes her eyes, gritting her teeth.

The saw finally reaches her and hoses her face with a geyser of blood. Screaming until she's hoarse, Bug steadily feeds her arm through the furiously spinning blade. The tissue separates as though it were merely damp paper.

Next, the tough of her bone. The saw screeches, sputtering, as it starts to chew through her muscle.

Bug screams, the very last of the threads of tissue loosening from the blood-buttered tendon with a squelching sound.

Finally, the arm snaps.

When Bird finds her hours later, she does not find the blood, nor the agony Bug had endured to transform herself so remarkably. Instead, Bird finds a goddess.

Bug stands on the table in a shaft of golden light, the saw still spinning beneath her.

Both of her arms have been severed. But no blood.

She stands unmoving—an immaculately poised, armless torso. A statue.

The paleness of her skin shimmers in the light.

Her reddish hair—pulled back in a diamond-embellished bun at the back of her head.

Naked, except for a transparent silk robe draped about her waist.

A gentle gust of wind permanently surrounds her, lifting the edges of her robe and teasing the loose threads of hair dangling about her face.

The light sharpens. Even the air around her glitters as if she had managed to enchant that as well.

When Bird reaches the foot of the table, her eyes lower and find her. Her face warms with a smile.

She opens her mouth to speak. The warmth of her breath sparkles in the light.

"I almost couldn't finish," Bug tells her wife.

Bird lets the razor slip from her hands.

It's not long before her blank stare turns to admiration. She clears the catch in her throat.

"Beautiful," Bird says.

Bug steps down from the table. A soft blast of air follows her glowing body as she moves.

Bird steps into the shaft of light circling Bug, her mouth hanging open. She reaches out to her, and her trembling fingers move from her eyes to her lips.

Bird presses her lips against Bug's.

They kneel together, and Bird lays Bug on the floor like a precious newborn. She lies beside her.

Eyes still closed; Bug's face softens.

"What do we say—?"

Bird presses her face against Bug's, mouth caressing her ear.

"Bird eats Bug."

"Bug feeds Bird."

The panel of ceiling lights overhead flashes for a moment.

Bug closes her eyes.

When she opens her eyes, the golden halo around her flickers out and vanishes.

She's alone on the cellar floor. Bird is nowhere in sight.

Her right arm—still attached; her left, however, completely severed and lying beside her on the ground, fountaining blood all over the floor.

The table saw continues to spin, sprinkling the walls of the cellar with her blood—her wants, her desires, her most shameful and wanton secrets.

Bug strains to lift her head and regards her right arm—still in its proper place.

She winces, lifting her blood-soaked body and tucking her still-attached right arm behind her back until she resembles the limbless torso she had so desperately strained to imitate.

Bug's body loosens as a blast of air embraces and cradles her.

Smiling, her eyes sparkle.

Perfection.

Gently, she breathes:

"Bird and Bug are happy."

71

When It's Dark Out

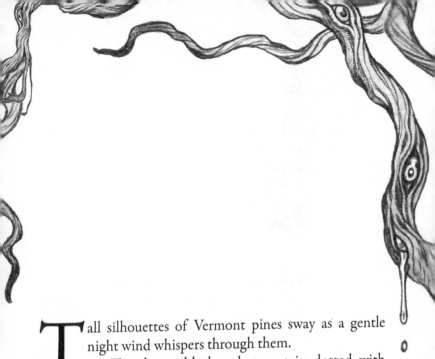

Tall silhouettes of Vermont pines sway as a gentle night wind whispers through them.

The sky—a black, velvet curtain dotted with glittering specks of tin foil.

A pair of car headlights crown the head of the hill and dip down the narrow ribbon of empty roadway like two floating paper lanterns.

The car slows, hazard lights blinking, and slips on to the tree-flanked shoulder as it creeps to a stop.

Marcus Dove, a pockmark-faced man in his early 40's, lifts himself out of the car and steps onto the roadway.

He wipes beads of sweat from his forehead. A dark-red band of skin dotted with rusted grains of blood runs from his temple to below his right eye. The wound—about a week old and disguised with dressings.

He opens the rear passenger door to reveal his eight-year-old son, Julian.

Dressed in pajamas, Julian stirs.

The interior light overhead him illuminates the glassy film of blindness dimming both of the boy's eyes.

"Where is it—?" Marcus asks, searching the backseat.

Julian winces a little. "He's scared."

"Julian. Now."

Julian opens his cupped hands to reveal a small snake. Its tail thrashing gently, its little body the color of licorice.

"Hugo's not dangerous," Julian insists. "The man at the pet store said he wasn't."

Marcus shakes his head, unconvinced. "I don't want that *thing* in the car, Jules."

Julian's head lowers, as if shamed. "He has a name."

"Julian."

"I just thought Dad might like to see him again."

Marcus' face stiffens with a somber look at the horrible reminder.

"We're going to be late," Marcus reminds his son.

"Please," Julian begs. "I'll keep him in my pocket for the rest of the ride. I promise."

But Marcus won't accept it. He holds out his hand. "Now."

Just then, Marcus realizes he'll have to actually hold the little creature.

"Wait," he says, dipping his head through the window of the front seat and grabbing a small tissue. He returns to Julian and holds his open palm out with the tissue blanketing his hand.

"OK. Now," he says.

Julian's lip slackens. "No. Let me do it."

He reaches over to the seat next to him and gropes for his white cane.

"It's too dark," Marcus tells him.

Julian looks at his father, insulted. After all, his whole world has been dark.

"Marcus," Julian says, folding his arms.

Marcus realizes. "Right."

Marcus lifts his son out of the car.

With one hand guiding the white cane and the other holding the small snake, Julian begins to inch away from the car.

"You can't let it go here?" Marcus asks.

"And let him get squished?"

Marcus takes Julian's arm, guiding him. Julian shrugs away.

Julian shuffles further off while Marcus remains at the car. After several steps, the boy reaches a small clearing of grass before a thicket.

He gets down on both knees, holding Hugo in his hand. He whispers to him.

"Sorry about Marcus," he says to his pet snake. "He didn't mean what he said. The part about you being disgusting, I mean ... And sorry for bringing it up again ... He doesn't like most things. Sometimes, I think I'm one of the things he doesn't like. My other dad, too. He didn't start kissing him until he got to the hospital last month. Too bad he's always sleeping when he does it now."

Marcus, wiping his face with a washcloth, calls out to Julian from the car.

"Jules," he says.

Julian's lip crumples, eyes closing as he hugs Hugo tightly.

"Dad would let me keep you," he says to the small snake. "You're a nice monster. Like me."

Julian slips Hugo into his pocket and rises.

Marcus waits for him at the car.

"He'll be okay," Marcus tells his son.

Julian's face softens a little with a smile.

"You said 'he.'"

Then Marcus helps his son into the backseat and shuts

the door. He shifts the gear, and the car launches forward, ambling back onto the empty roadway.

The car headlights dim as they disappear farther down the lane, swallowed by the gaping maw of dark.

With both hands on the wheel, Marcus' eyes move from the road ahead to the rearview mirror. Julian's head is slightly lowered, his body without movement.

Marcus shifts in his seat, clearing his throat.

"Music?" he asks.

But Julian won't answer.

"Jules."

"No thank you," the boy says.

More silence follows.

"I can pull over," Marcus says. "Let you sit in the front."

"That's okay."

"You always ask to."

"When Dad's here," Julian says.

Marcus glances in the rearview mirror and notices he looks both nervous and upset.

"You don't want to see your present then?"

Julian stirs in his seat.

"Present?"

Marcus smiles.

"Now you're reconsidering—?"

Marcus reaches under the passenger seat beside him and draws out a box. He hands it to Julian.

Julian lifts the lid and reaches inside, pulling out a walkie-talkie. His fingers run over the object.

"What is it—?"

"It's a walkie-talkie. One for you. One for me."

Julian takes out the second walkie-talkie, holding both of them in his hands.

Marcus inhales deeply.

"I may not always answer. But I promise I'll always hear you."

"You promise you'll always keep it with you? Even when you go away on your trips?"

Panic flushes Marcus' face. It's a promise he knows he cannot keep.

"I promise," he whispers.

Julian hands Marcus one of the devices.

Marcus brings his walkie-talkie close to his ear. Julian pushes a button and presses his mouth against the microphone.

"Hi, Marcus."

Julian laughs.

"Hi, Jules."

Marcus smiles.

"Marcus ... "

Marcus' face hardens, as if expecting something unpleasant.

"Yeah?"

"You're not going to take any more trips, are you?"

Marcus draws the walkie-talkie away from his ear, tucking it in his pocket.

"We have the walkie-talkies now," he says. "So, it doesn't even matter if I'm gone for a while."

"They don't work more than a couple of miles."

Marcus pales.

His eyes return to the road.

His eyebrows arch and his lips tighten as he sees something float up in front of the headlights of the car—a black balloon tied to a silver thread.

The balloon bobs up in front of the lights and floats up in front of the grill, up above the car and out of Marcus' sight.

He lowers his head to look up beyond the roof of the car.

"Why are we going?" Julian asks.

"Going—?"

"To the hospital."

"We're going to see Dad," Marcus explains.

"He's always sleeping."

Marcus' lip pulls downward. His voice rough, as though his throat were filled with rotted flowers.

"I know."

"We never go this late."

"We're going to say, 'good night.'"

"Are we going to say, 'good night' to him every night?" Julian asks.

Marcus' lips part, unsure what to say.

"No," he says. "Just tonight."

As Marcus' eyes return to the road, he slams both feet on the brakes and shouts.

Something shiny and round flickers, disappearing beneath the headlights as the entire car lifts.

Wheels screech as they spin over something lying in the middle of the road.

A wet, crunching sound.

The car buckles as it claps down on the pavement and skids to a stop.

Marcus' hands do not leave the steering wheel. Mouth open in disbelief, his breath whistles.

"Jules. Are you okay?" he asks.

"What—what was it?"

Marcus turns his head gently, adjusting his glasses.

"I—don't know."

Marcus' eyes fill with dread. His hand fumbles in the

glove compartment, grabbing a flashlight, before he opens the door. With trembling legs, he steps out of the car and onto the pavement.

Marcus turns mechanically back toward the thing behind the idling car.

"Please be an animal. Please be an animal."

A black balloon tied to a glistening thread floats at his eye level. Its oily surface—leathery like embalmed flesh and dappled with bulging veins.

Marcus slowly approaches, aiming the flashlight.

It's then that he finally sees what the thread of the balloon is tied to—a steaming pile of human viscera.

Thin coils of red-and-flesh-colored stripes scarcely covered by a tattered shirt and pair of dress pants.

Covering his mouth, he staggers over a pair of black loafers.

He rushes to the side of the road and vomits.

He doesn't notice his cellphone slip from his pocket, vanishing into the tall grass.

Julian calls him from inside the car:

"Marcus—?"

Wiping wet strands of vomit from his lips, Marcus staggers back toward the remains.

"Don't come out here," he barks at his son.

His eyes dart all around him. He thinks he hears an approaching car. His body tenses, head swiveling back and forth.

Marcus pulls out a tissue from his pocket and covers his nose and mouth as he kneels beside the remains. He frowns, unable to resist examining the mess.

His face scrunches with disgust as his hands reach out and gently lift a moist ribbon of flattened tissue from the pile of shredded anatomy. He pinches it between his thumb and pointer finger. The ribbon whispers tiny wreaths of heat.

He recoils, the slippery band of skin slipping from between his fingers. Lurching backwards on hands and knees, his head slams into the bumper of the car.

Cupping his head, Marcus then notices the blood smeared on his fingers. He springs up and rushes to the front passenger seat.

He opens the door and grabs the bottle of hand sanitizer on the seat, emptying it into his trembling hands.

Julian stirs in the backseat, head revolving.

"What was it—?"

"Stay there," Marcus shouts. "Don't move."

Marcus slams the door shut and moves back behind the car again.

The flashlight shaking in his hand, he checks both rear tires—lines of soaking redness, flecks of tissue shimmering in the grooves.

He wipes the tire with his cloth as blood drips on his shoes.

Marcus scurries to the backseat door, flinging it open.

"What is it—?" Julian asks.

An idea creeps into Marcus' mind. "A deer. I—saw it crawl back into the woods."

"Should we make sure it's okay?" Julian asks.

Marcus slams Julian's door. He flings open the driver's door and throws himself behind the steering wheel.

Marcus shifts the car into DRIVE, the car revving sweetly and tearing down the road.

Julian stirs in the backseat.

"Marcus—?"

But Marcus doesn't answer.

His feet push down hard on the gas pedal, the car accelerating.

"Shut up. Let me think," he tells his son.

Eyes darting back and forth between the roadway ahead and the vanishing remains in the rearview mirror, Marcus slams his fists against the steering wheel.

"FUCK," he shouts.

"Did you—kill it—?" the frightened boy asks him.

"Shut up."

Julian bites his lip, choking on quiet sobs.

Suddenly, Marcus sees a row of lights in the roadway up ahead.

A one-lane toll booth.

He eases on the breaks, the car slowing to a crawl as they approach.

Eyes narrowing to mere slits, he sees a black SUV parked and idling beside the toll booth.

Marcus taps on the brakes until he parks behind the loitering vehicle.

He shakes his head, noticing the driver's door has been left opened and the hazard lights flashing.

His eyes scan the dimly lit toll booth. Nothing.

He lays on the horn, shouting:

"HEY!"

Julian jumps, startled by the noise.

Marcus rolls down the window, craning his head out.

"Hello—?"

Silence.

Unbuckling his seat belt, he adjusts the rearview mirror until Julian's pout comes into view.

"Stay here," he tells Julian.

Marcus pulls the door handle, hoisting himself out of the driver's seat.

The light above the toll booth flickers, hissing and bathing the road in a dim, emerald glow.

Marcus meanders from behind the humming parked car, eyes peering through empty windows.

When he reaches the opened driver's door, he finds the ground hosed with blood. Ribbons of skin and tissue hang from the door handle.

He follows the streaks of redness smeared with footprints to the toll booth door. The glass—caked with a bloody handprint—spiderwebs in tiny cracks.

Marcus pushes the door open until it creaks.

A boy's voice calls to him from inside the booth.

"Help—me," the voice says.

Marcus recoils, covering his mouth at the sight.

He sees a dark-haired, pockmark-faced teenager huddled beneath a desk. The boy clutches what appears to be a severed, blood-soaked arm.

"Please," the teenager begs. "Get me out of here."

Marcus trembles, staggering back.

"Wha-what happened-?"

Without warning, a vulgar thud slams against the roof of the toll booth. The tiny building shakes, lights dimming.

The sound of talons screeching, claws being dragged across metal.

An inhuman moan. The deafening thunder of wings beating. The wet, slapping sound of tentacles curling about the sides of the building.

"Close the door," the teenager says. "Get down."

Marcus drags the door shut, locking it. He crouches on the ground, crawling toward the teenager.

His head swivels, eyes nervously darting from window to window.

A giant dark shape flits past the window.

A violent hiss of wind. Another inhuman moan.

Marcus' knees buckle, and he grabs ahold of the chair.

"Julian," he whispers to himself, heading for the toll booth door.

"Don't go," the teenager says.

"My son's out there," Marcus explains.

The teenager shakes his head, voice trembling. "He's already dead."

Marcus lifts his weight on both knees, heaving himself toward the door.

"What are you?" the teenager asks. "Fucking mental? Don't open the door. It'll come in here."

"What is it? An animal—?"

"It didn't even touch me," the teenager says. "I saw it in a mirror for a second."

Marcus' eyes are drawn to the young boy's severed arm. "Your arm," he says.

"Turned it to fucking string, man."

Marcus slowly approaches the teenager, his foot slipping on a wet ribbon of skin coiled on the ground like a dozing snake.

Marcus lifts the poor boy's blood-soaked shirt sleeve, inspecting his arm. He covers his mouth, grimacing.

"You've—lost a lot of blood," Marcus says.

"Lost a lot of blood?" the teenager shouts at him. "My arm's a fucking unraveled Christmas sweater!"

Marcus retches at the sight—a shining, blistered stump where the boy's extremity once was. The ivory fishhook of his bone sequined in an elastic cushion of oily sinew.

He doubles over, vomiting in his hands.

The boy covers his mouth, groaning, at the stench.

"Dude. That fucking stinks," he says.

Marcus wipes his wet hands on a coat draped over the desk chair.

He reaches in his pocket. No cell phone. He pats his shirt pockets. Nothing.

"Fuck."

"Stay down," the teenager says. "It'll see you."

"We—have to get you out of here," Marcus tells him.

"And let that—thing—finish what it started?" the boy asks. "Fuck no."

"You'll die if we don't," Marcus tells him. "Where's your phone?"

"Left it in my car."

"I think I remember a gas station a mile up ahead..."

The teenager inches further beneath the desk, cowering. "Someone else will come along."

"And have them stuck in here with us too?" Marcus asks.

"I didn't wait long until you showed up," the teenager explains. "Someone will find us."

"Where's the guy that works here?" Marcus asks him.

The boy shudders, about to retch again. "All he did was— look at the thing. Then. Fucking string cheese, man."

"Did he—wear black loafers?" Marcus asks.

The boy merely shrugs.

"I think—I just peeled parts of him off my tire," Marcus says.

The teenager thinks for a moment. "... Probably for the best."

Marcus straightens one of his legs, peering out of the toll booth window.

Just then, Marcus remembers. He fishes inside his shirt pocket and slips out the walkie-talkie.

Marcus turns the dial, flicks a button, and holds his mouth close to the speaker.

"Julian. Jules."

Finally, Julian responds:

"Marcus—?"

Marcus' face relaxes. He exhales.

"Jules. Thank God," he says.

"Where are you?" his son asks him.

"I'm—coming back," Marcus assures him. "I promise. Are you OK?"

"Something's on top of the car," his son tells him.

Fuck, Marcus thinks to himself.

He speaks into the walkie-talkie: "Jules. I need you to listen carefully. I need you to feel in the front seat for my phone. Can you do that?"

A long pause.

"I can't find it," Julian says.

"You checked everywhere?"

Another long pause while the young boy searches for the phone.

"It's not here," he tells his father.

"Jules. I'm—"

"Coming back. I promise," Julian says, mimicking a phrase he's heard time and time again.

"Jules," Marcus says.

But Julian won't answer this time.

Marcus exhales, eyes closed.

"I'm sorry," he whispers, hoping Julian might hear him.

Outside the toll booth—the sound of wings thrashing. An inhuman howl.

The teenager sits with his back propped up against the desk. His damp sleeve has been tied and fastened into a makeshift tourniquet.

Marcus sits across from him. He stirs gently, head craning up and out of the toll booth window.

"You want to get us both killed—?" the teenager asks him.

"My son," Marcus says gently. Then stops himself.

"How old is he—?" the young man asks him.

Marcus opens his mouth to answer, but stops.

"You don't remember?"

"Of course, I remember," Marcus says to him, visibly insulted. "Eight. Next month... No. Eight candles on the cake last year. So... Nine. Next month... His father's better with birthdays."

The teenager's face scrunches at him. "You're—not his father—?"

"His *other* father," Marcus explains.

The teenager's expression changes from concern to disgust.

"Oh. So, you're a—?"

Marcus' face hardens, lips crinkling, as if daring the teenager to say the word.

"A what?" he asks him.

"That's cool," the teenager says. "I thought about being gay for a while. Girls love gay dudes. Take 'em shopping. Let 'em sit in the dressing rooms while they change. I'd be into that."

Marcus rolls his eyes.

"You have to learn the secret handshake first," he says, amusing himself.

"What is it?" the teenager asks him.

Marcus glares at him, incredulous.

The teenager's face crumples, disgusted.

"You mean with your—dicks?" he says.

Marcus makes a noise of disgust, turning away. He peers out the window quickly before ducking out of sight once more.

"I'm guessing you—adopted," the young sullen boy says.

"My husband told me the day after we were married all he wanted was to have a house in the country and raise a kid."

"I'm sure Norman Rockwell would've loved to paint that," the teenager teases.

Marcus ignores the boy's hateful comment. He clears the dampness in his eyes, shaking his head.

"I'm—afraid of what he'll think of me one day," Marcus says. "When he realizes. He's already asked why he doesn't have a mom like the other kids at school. I'll have to be the one to tell him. His father—won't be around."

"Why?" the teenager asks him.

Marcus clears the dampness in both eyes. He shakes his head.

"We were on our way to see him tonight—one last time. He's in the hospital."

The teenager leans in close, his face hardening with concern.

"AIDS?"

Marcus could spit on him. He throws him a look of disgust.

"No. You asshole."

"Sorry. Honest question. What happened—?"

Marcus glances away, clearing the catch in his throat.

"We were driving to—pick our son up from school. Arguing. As usual."

"About—?"

"The kid," Marcus says. "It's always about the kid. It's his fault. Never mind. I—shouldn't have been driving. I was—angry."

"He stuck it in your ass too quick—?"

Marcus turns slowly, facing the teenager. His lips purse with a snarl.

"What did you say—?"

But the teenager is too busy laughing, far too amused with himself, far too distracted by his utter cruelty.

Meanwhile, in the car outside the toll booth, Julian sits with his head lowered. He's asleep in the backseat.

A faint scratching on the roof of the car. A soft moan—an otherworldly wail of anguish. A delicate rustling of wings.

Something unseen shifts its massive weight from one side of the roof to the other, the car rocking gently.

Julian yawns, stretching awake.

His hands pat the seat beside him. He can't find Hugo.

"Hugo—?" he says.

Julian's body stiffens, panicking as his hands beat against the leather seats to search for his snake.

He unlocks the car door and opens it.

Unbeknownst to him, Hugo sneaks out from underneath Julian's seat and falls out of the car, slithering onto the pavement.

Julian's ears perk at the sound of Hugo's tiny body on the move. He fumbles nervously about to no avail.

"Hugo," the boy calls out.

Another inhuman moan responds.

Julian drags the door shut. He pants, ducking into the space behind the front the seat.

A black balloon tied to a silver thread floats past the vehicle. It sways, bobbing at Julian's window. Veins pulse along the object's fleshy surface, and it inflates and deflates as if it were a giant lung.

Although Julian can't see the balloon, his ears perk at the sound of its squealing as it rubs against the car. He tilts his head, trying to comprehend.

Without warning, the balloon pops.

Julian covers his ears.

Black sludge hoses the window, splattering against the glass like hot hail. Glistening threads curl like small tentacles, dripping down the car door.

Marcus straightens his knees, lifting slightly and peering out the window. Nothing. He turns back to the teenager.

"You can help yourself, you shit," he says. "If you're not coming, I'll go on my own."

The teenager eyes Marcus as if he were mere prey.

"So. Your special guy ..."

Marcus turns away, crawling toward the door.

"I don't want to talk about it. Not to you."

Marcus stops. His eyes glisten with wetness.

"He's going to—die?"

Marcus closes his eyes, shaking his head.

"They're—taking him off life support tonight," Marcus explains.

The teenager suddenly grins from ear to ear, wheezing with laughter.

"I heard you can get a boner in a coma," he says. "You think there are nurses in charge of—relieving—patients?"

Marcus rolls his eyes. The teenager giggles.

"I'm sure they'd give your husband a male nurse."

Marcus finally explodes. "What the fuck is your problem, you little twat?"

The teenager looks around the small room, as if appraising whether or not they're in immediate danger.

"Have you wondered if that thing can hear us?" he asks Marcus. "The louder you are. The hungrier it gets."

"What are you saying?" Marcus asks.

"You're the one leading it toward dinner."

"You're trying to get a rise out of me on purpose?" Marcus asks, slowly realizing.

"That thing wants to eat."

"You'd be leading it to you too, idiot," Marcus says, spitting at him.

The teenager opens his mouth for a rebuttal, but he has no words.

"Thank God Julian isn't the little shit you are," Marcus says.

"You still hate him."

Marcus turns, face paling.

"What—?"

"Your kid. Don't you—?"

Marcus, flustered, stammers.

"He's—"

"A pain in your ass," the teenager says, finishing the sentence for him. "And even though you're used to that, you still hate him."

Marcus snarls, clenching his fists.

"SHUT UP."

"All parents hate their kids sometimes," the sullen boy says. "My stepdad hated me."

Marcus rolls his eyes. "Even with all your charm?"

"It's okay," the boy says. "I hated him, too. What I don't get is why he married my mom if he hated her, too. He's friends with cops. So, what do they do? They pretend they don't see the bruises on her arms and legs."

Marcus senses his face softening.

"I'm sorry."

The teenager's eyes suddenly light up with an idea.

"Hey. Where's that walkie-talkie?"

Marcus grips the walkie-talkie, reluctant. "What are you going to do?"

The teenager snatches the device from Marcus' hands. He presses his lips against the speaker, holding down the small button to talk.

"Hey—what's your kid's name?" he asks Marcus.

"Julian. We call him 'Jules' sometimes."

The teenager shouts into the walkie-talkie: "Jules, this is your dad's new friend. Are you there?"

"Yeah," Julian responds.

"Good boy," the teenager says. "Can you do me a favor, buddy? Reach up to the front seat and turn on the car radio."

Marcus leans in closer. "What are you doing—?"

"Turn the volume up as loud as you can. And get out of the car," the teenager orders Julian.

Marcus snatches the walkie-talkie from him.

"What the fuck are you doing?" he asks him.

"Solving both of our problems," the teenager explains.

"Jules, don't listen to him," Marcus yells into the walkie-talkie. Then he corners the teenager. "You're a fucking monster."

"Is it going to be him? Or us?" the teenager asks Marcus.

Marcus lunges at the boy, grabbing his throat and squeezing.

"You fucking piece of shit."

Marcus drags the teenager's body to the door, unlocking it.

He opens the toll booth door, heaving half of the boy's body over the threshold.

"Another death on your conscience?" the teenager asks him.

Marcus stops, eyes never leaving the boy. His lips quiver with soundless words.

"You're not a monster," the boy tells him.

Marcus' grip on the teenager begins to loosen, his face softening.

Just then, the snake crawls beside the teenager's shoulder and slithers inside the toll booth. The boy screams, lurching up and dragging himself out.

His arm flails, furiously patting himself as he staggers into the road.

Realizing the snake is gone, his body quiets to stillness. His eyes arrive at Marcus standing inside the toll booth.

Marcus immediately shuts the entrance, locking it.

The teenager rushes to the door, pulling on the handle.

"Let me in, you fucking faggot," he shouts at him.

Marcus recoils, crouching on the floor to wait.

The teenager turns. He sees something flicker in the darkness beyond the island of light.

Without warning, a black balloon appears and floats toward him. His feet are glued to the ground; he merely watches it.

The balloon's needle-thin thread curls into a glistening hook and stabs his chest, a burst of blood exploding and shaking his body as if he were a rag doll.

The balloon pops, black sludge hosing his face. He shudders, screaming.

Marcus watches as the poor boy convulses, hand furiously wiping his eyes and mouth.

A giant shape descends upon the teenager, the shadow swallowing him in darkness. The sounds of the creature sniffing him and inhaling deeply.

Marcus covers his mouth as he watches as a thread of skin lift from the boy's hand, coiling in the air as if it were a charmed snake. Suddenly, more threads of skin begin to unravel from his body until ribbons of skin and viscera flurry about him like a snow squall.

Marcus turns away, closing his eyes, as the teenager screams.

Marcus gropes about the floor for the walkie-talkie. Grabbing it, he presses the button to speak.

"Jules. Are you there?" he asks.

"Marcus," Julian responds.

"Are you hurt?"

"Something's moving by the car."

"Can it see you?"

"It's right by the window."

Marcus crawls to the toll booth door. He unlocks it, pushing it open a few inches. Craning his head out, he observes his parked car in the reflection of the glass door.

A giant dark shape looms beside the parked car.

He sees his son's face in the window, eyes staring blankly out. Suddenly, the shape swallows the vehicle in darkness.

Marcus, peering through the crack in the toll booth door, watches helplessly with an open mouth as the giant figure heaves its weight against the vehicle and moans like a dying animal.

He sees Julian cower and cover his ears, but somehow the boy remains unharmed.

The sounds of the unseen creature shifting, snorting.

"It's—not ..."

Without warning, a black balloon flies at the toll booth door, tapping at it with a shiny hooked stinger and hosing the glass with fluid.

Black sludge splatters on Marcus' hand before he can shut the door. He cries out, locking the handle.

He closes his eyes, body shuddering, as the dark shape passes in front of the glass door. Its shadow looms over him for a moment, tentacles thrashing at the door with moist, slapping sounds.

Then, it passes, disappearing.

Panting like a feral dog in heat, Marcus slowly opens his eyes.

He sees a silvery flash of the creature's tail reflected in the glass door.

A thread of skin lifts from his index finger and begins to unspool as if his skin were yarn. Exposed sinew lifts and unravels as well.

He stares, mouth open in disbelief, at the blistered nub where his index finger once was.

Marcus eyes the remains of the boy in the roadway. The balloon bobbing in the wind, its silvery thread still hooked to a thread of the teenager's confetti viscera.

"He—looked—at it," Marcus says to himself.

Suddenly, the walls of the toll booth shake, the roof creaking, as if something enormous had just slammed into it.

An overhead panel of lights inside the booth snaps from its cables and crashes to the floor, shattering.

Marcus ducks as sparks burst, livid dots of fire exploding from the shattered remains.

Marcus clutches the walkie-talkie.

"Julian. Are you still there?"

"Marcus—?"

"Stay there. I'm coming to get you," Marcus promises him.

Marcus clicks the walkie-talkie off.

A trail of fire blazes from the light panel to the wiring fixed on top of the booth operator's desk.

On hands and knees, he crawls about the floor of the toll booth, head craning beneath cabinets as he searches.

Finally, he finds what he's been looking for—Hugo.

Tucked behind a small file cabinet, Hugo recoils, his tail curling and threatening to strike.

Marcus pinches the tiny creature and drags him out from beneath his hiding place.

Flames flicker, inhaling more of the tiny room.

Marcus regards Hugo for a moment as he removes his glasses.

He plucks Hugo, his index finger and thumb hugging his body.

Hugo's tiny tail flails helplessly as Marcus drags him in the air.

Without a second thought, Marcus aims Hugo's fang at his lidless right eye and drives him into it, the tiny needle stabbing him.

His eyelids flutter madly, eyes watering. He screams.

Before resolve abandons him completely, he finishes the final task—his left eye. He hurls Hugo at his eye, Hugo's fangs stabbing him again and again.

Marcus blinks, his throat choked with whimpers.

He staggers forward, eyes closed, and crashes into the burning desk.

The fire roars, curtains of smoke swallowing Marcus until he rushes the door and flies out of the toll booth.

Marcus staggers outside, coughing and cradling Hugo. He slams into the parked SUV.

The toll booth windows glow brightly and, without warning, explode as flames snarl and lick the walls like waves.

Marcus hastens blindly toward his parked car. He gropes about the vehicle.

"Jules," he calls out.

His hands nervously run down the length of the car—from the hood to the backseat passenger door. His fingers find the handle and he pulls.

Julian, crouching on the floor, stirs gently.

Marcus pats the seat for his son. Hands finding his boy, he pulls him close to his chest.

He leans down, his lips finding his son's forehead and pecking him with a kiss.

Marcus grabs Julian's hand, opening his fingers to make a small bowl. He spoons Hugo from his palm and into Julian's hand.

"You found him," the little boy says.

Julian's face thaws. His voice—a mere whimper. "Thanks—Dad."

Marcus smiles, his eyes swollen shut.

"Let's go," he says.

Julian slides Hugo into his pocket and pats the seat for his walking cane, grabbing it before his father scoops him out of his seat.

Julian taps the ground with the end of his cane, uncertain. Marcus grabs his hand tightly.

"Where are we going?" the boy asks his father.

"You lead," Marcus tells him. "I'll follow."

Julian shifts forward, tapping the road as he walks. Marcus inches behind his son, their hands locked together.

The toll booth growls with waves of fire—a shimmering inferno.

A giant shadow passes over Marcus and Julian as they meander toward oblivion—two small specks glinting in a seemingly infinite ocean of darkness.

Without warning, a deafening wail blasts pine needles from nearby trees, showering them in a glittery hailstorm.

A black balloon, its silver thread glistening, follows father and son until their shapes move beyond the flickering glow of fire and vanish into the dark ahead.

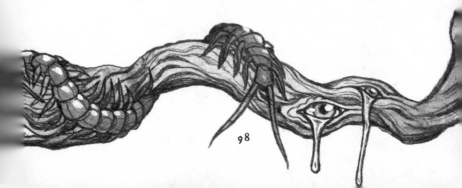

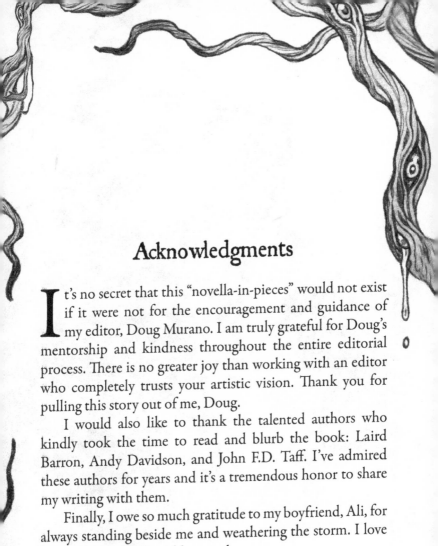

Acknowledgments

It's no secret that this "novella-in-pieces" would not exist if it were not for the encouragement and guidance of my editor, Doug Murano. I am truly grateful for Doug's mentorship and kindness throughout the entire editorial process. There is no greater joy than working with an editor who completely trusts your artistic vision. Thank you for pulling this story out of me, Doug.

I would also like to thank the talented authors who kindly took the time to read and blurb the book: Laird Barron, Andy Davidson, and John F.D. Taff. I've admired these authors for years and it's a tremendous honor to share my writing with them.

Finally, I owe so much gratitude to my boyfriend, Ali, for always standing beside me and weathering the storm. I love you so much that I could unravel.

About the Author

ERIC LAROCCA (he/they) is the Bram Stoker Award®-nominated author of several works of horror and dark fiction including the viral sensation Things Have Gotten Worse Since We Last Spoke. A lover of luxury fashion and an admirer of European musical theatre, Eric can often be found roaming the streets of his home city, Boston, MA, for inspiration. For more information, please follow @hystericteeth on Twitter/Instagram or visit ericlarocca.com.